Shelter of Daylight
May 2025

Features

63   The Protocol: A Book Review by Alan Ira Gordon

Short Stories

10   In These Hands by Lawrence Buentello

33   Close to the Wind by Gustavo Bondoni

66   Love After Death by Paul Lonardo

Flash Fiction

50   Trixie by K. S. Hardy

55   Tin Can by Debby Feo

THE STAFF OF SHELTER OF DAYLIGHT:

MANAGING EDITOR: Tyree Campbell
WEBMASTER: H David Blalock

Cover art "Brighde" by Paula Hammond
Cover design by Marcia A. Borell

Vol. VI, No. 2   May 2025

Shelter of Daylight is published three times a year, on the 1st days of January, May, and September in the United States of America by Hiraeth Publishing, P.O. Box 1248, Tularosa, NM 88352. Copyright 2025 by Hiraeth Publishing. All rights revert to authors and artists upon publication except as noted in selected individual contracts. Nothing may be reproduced in whole or in part without written permission from the authors and artists. Any similarity between places and persons mentioned in the fiction or semi-fiction and real places or persons living or dead is coincidental. Writers and artists guidelines are available online at www.hiraethsffh.com. Guidelines are also available upon request from Hiraeth Publishing, P.O. Box 1248, Tularosa, NM 88352, if request is accompanied by a self-addressed #10 envelope with a first-class US stamp. Editor: Tyree Campbell.

Protect your First Amendment Rights! Support the Small Independent Press!

A Little Help, Please

In the world of the small indie press we fight a never-ending battle for attention to our work, as writers and in publishing. Here's an example: big publishers [you know who they are] have gobs of $$$ that they can devote to advertising and marketing. Here at Hiraeth Publishing, our advertising budget consists of the deposits for whatever soda bottles and aluminum cans we can find alongside the highways. Anti-littering laws make our task even more difficult . . . ☺

That's where YOU come in. YOU are our best promoter. YOU are the one who can tell others about us. Just send 'em to our website, tell them about our store. That's all. Just that.

Of course, we don't mind if you talk us up. We're pretty good, you know. We have some award-winning and award-nominated writers and artists, plus other voices well-deserving to be heard [not everyone wins awards, right?] but our publications are read-worthy nevertheless.

That number once again is:

www.hiraethsffh.com

Friend us on Facebook at Hiraeth Publish
Follow us on Twitter at
@ HiraethPublish1

New from Hiraeth Publishing!!
The Future Adventures of
Bailey Belvedere

As the societies of Earth collapse into chaos and destruction, Bailey Belvedere, a U.S. Army Intelligence officer fighting for her very survival, steals aboard an alien spacecraft, and soon finds herself given the authority and power by a superior alien entity to intervene in various problems in the Galaxy. Along the way she frees a world from interstellar slave traffickers, deals with an AI who becomes pregnant, inadvertently destroys a waffle house, fights against the abductors of a special child, and generally finds herself in some sort of trouble from one moment to the next.

Type: Novel – science fiction

Ordering Link:
Print Edition:
https://www.hiraethsffh.com/product-page/further-adventures-of-bailey-belvedere-by-tyree-campbell

PDF Edition: https://www.hiraethsffh.com/product-page/further-adventures-of-bailey-belvedere-by-tyree-campbell-1

The Oculist's Daughter
By Angel Favazza

The Oculist's Daughter by Angel Favazza is a steampunker in the old west. It's got a semi-mad scientist (her dad), her, of course, plus outlaws, Indians, Wyoming, a poison gas for killing natives, and an Indian guide. It all adds up to a rollicking adventure.

https://www.hiraethsffh.com/product-page/oculist-s-daughter-by-angel-favazza

Wearing Winter Gray

Atmospheric poetry at its finest is found in Wearing Winter Gray. Lee Clark Zumpe sets his moods and draws forth evocative images and memories, and not a little emotion. Now and then a ray of light shines through his words, so that having created a somber mood, he punctuates it with a bit of joy. Thus it is that Wearing Winter Gray reminds us that Shiny Summer Colors are just around the corner.

Print: https://www.hiraethsffh.com/product-page/wearing-winter-gray-by-lee-clark-zumpe
ePub: https://www.hiraethsffh.com/product-page/wearing-winter-gray-by-lee-clark-zumpe-2
PDF: https://www.hiraethsffh.com/product-page/wearing-winter-gray-by-lee-clark-zumpe-1

Starwinders: Nohana's Heart

The scion of a corporate hierarch, Angrboda Vigdisdottir (Ayvy) wants to hijack a gold shipment to prevent an interstellar war. Disgraced security operative Pol Cahill is the ideal partner for her, given his skill set. Unfortunately, personalities clash. Finally, on a remote world, the two encounter one another in a tavern, and find that a young woman named Nohana, intensely educated and with a desire to travel among the stars, takes to the pair.

But the personalities continue to clash even as plans are laid to steal the gold. Nohana fills the power vacuum and becomes the so-called adult in the room. But Cahill is shot and wounded before they can carry out their plan. Nohana now has no choice but to try to save the day, despite her lack of experience. Meanwhile, the war awaits.

Ordering links:
Print: https://www.hiraethsffh.com/product-page/starwinders-nohana-s-heart-by-tyree-campbell

PDF: https://www.hiraethsffh.com/product-page/starwinders-1-nohana-s-heart-by-tyree-campbell

ePub: https://www.hiraethsffh.com/product-page/starwinders-1-nohana-s-heart-by-tyree-campbell-1

In These Hands
Lawrence Buentello

Night had fallen by the time Marco and his friends had gathered in the gloom of Macarthur Boulevard by the liquor store, between buildings, where no one would be foolish enough to investigate the depths of the shadows or the young men conversing quietly within their protection. The boulevard covered several miles, from quiet neighborhoods of houses to commercial urban sprawl; but the blocks on which they lived had been beaten down by age and poverty, left neglected by those who had themselves been neglected. The drunks were already beginning to migrate through the reinforced glass doors of the liquor store to purchase their supplies for the evening, liquor to be consumed in cheap apartments or familiar alleys; farther down the boulevard, dealers were beginning to populate side streets where users in cars would soon arrive to spend their money on an evening's escapism. Farther still, prostitutes were assembling on the sidewalks hoping for a busy night.

Marco, only sixteen, had no interest in dealing, at least, not then; Juan and Carlos were both seventeen, unaffiliated in the gangs, but not above petty theft when the opportunity arose. Marco, too, occasionally shoplifted, ambivalent over the concept of decency in a life spent enduring an indecent environment, though shoplifting seemed the least of his potential sins. His Mexican heritage wasn't an impediment on the streets, as long as he didn't invest his life in one of the Latin gangs, but he also couldn't see a future for himself. Not that he was unintelligent; he often visited the branch library several blocks away, reading for hours at a time, fascinated by history, literature, and science. Neither of his friends knew he visited the library, or that he even read many books, because they weren't interested in academics; they were just impoverished teenagers anticipating a life of unrewarding labor, or perhaps prison time if they didn't keep clean, or an early death if they were unable to avoid the gangs.

Carlos, burly and always in a bad mood, lit a cigarette, drew its tobacco into a dull glow, then said, "Let's walk."

Juan shook his head, his long black hair crowding his neck; Marco slipped his hands into the pockets of his black cloth jacket and pushed away from the wall he'd been leaning on. Together, they abandoned the shadows and began walking slowly down the sidewalk, pausing to stare into the windows of the stores, those still open and those already shut down for the day and gated against thieves.

"Does anyone have any money?" Carlos asked, bending to stare at day-old pastries through one of the windows. But no one had any money, so they moved on, gesturing toward the cars passing down the street, studying the shadows for faces which didn't belong in their neighborhood.

Before long, they stopped by an abandoned building which had burned from the inside out the year before, its windows and portals boarded, though drifters often found their way inside. Across the street, rising five stories, stood an old apartment house, more of a flop house now, a rusting fire escape zigzagging down its edifice like an immense scar, its windows either lighted by tenants or darkened against the sight of the street.

"Have you seen that old man?" Juan asked, pointing up toward one of the third floor windows.

Marco and Carlos followed Juan's gesture. Within the lighted window frame of one of the rooms, Marco caught sight of a figure sitting at a small table, his hands held before himself, palms up. Marco's eyesight, always exceptional, let him see the old man clearly—Black, with muscular arms, his close-cropped curly hair tinged with gray. The three young men stood watching the old man for a long time, but the old man only sat staring at his hands, never moving, as if in meditation.

Marco asked, "Have you seen him before?"

Juan rubbed his flat nose—broken in a fight in school—then said, "I've seen him a couple of times. Always sitting at that table, staring at his hands. He must be crazy."

Marco watched the old man for another moment, noting his sleeveless maroon shirt and shining eyes, a condition he'd seen in his grandfather's cataracted eyes before his death. The man's concentration seemed powerful, and Marco wondered what he contemplated as he sat before his window staring down on the decaying boulevard.

Carlos puffed on his cigarette one last time before flicking the smoldering butt into the street. "A lot of *loco* old men live in this neighborhood."

Juan laughed. "They're not *loco*, just burned out from too much whiskey. Like my father. *Desinteresado*. He never wants to be bothered by anyone or anything anymore. That's going to be us one day."

"We can't even afford to buy one bottle," Marco said, turning to glance at his friends before returning his attention to the old man in the window. "What's he doing?"

Carlos laughed. "Remembering the good old days."

"If he was on the street with us," Juan said, "would you ask him?"

Carlos shook his head. "No."

"Why not?"

"There's something strange about him. I don't know."

Juan stared up toward the window. "Very strange."

Marco ran his palm over his short black hair, mesmerized by the image of the old Black man in the window. He understood—he perceived, in some way, an aura the old man held, a feeling, a sensation of— What? But the longer he stood watching the old man, the greater the intensity of the feeling; it seemed as if he was staring at someone *more* than a man, which seemed an irrational thought.

Carlos lit another cigarette, then said, "Let's keep walking. It's a bad idea to stand in one place for too long."

Juan nodded, then turned.

Marco, still watching the figure in the window, heard his friend's suggestion but couldn't turn away. Then Carlos laid a strong hand on his shoulder and he finally broke free of his trance. As they ambled slowly down the sidewalk, though, he kept glancing back toward the building, until they'd walked too far for him to see its windows any longer.

* * *

After that night, Marco began returning to the burnt-out store front to study the old man. He didn't understand his motivation for wanting to do so, but it seemed a better use of his time than sitting in his own small apartment watching television with his mother and sisters, or arguing over one damned thing or another. His mother and his two sisters had their own bedrooms; at night, he slept on the sofa listening to the loud voices, the drunken voices echoing through the walls of the living room, wishing he could sleep in peace just one night. Some nights he'd hear his mother crying in her room, no doubt for the life she'd never lived, and he'd cover his ears with his hands.

On the third night, after several hours of surveillance, as he leaned back against a wall in the shadows, he observed the old man turn his head briefly from his meditation to gaze down toward the street, toward *him*, as if he could see Marco standing in shadows—and then the old man returned his focus to the empty space between his hands. Certainly he couldn't have seen Marco from that distance, not in darkness, not where he'd been standing. But he'd felt the power of the old man's stare, as if he'd fixed Marco and let him know he knew the boy stood watching him.

Marco, lost in thought, failed to notice Juan walking up to him on the street.

"Marco?" Juan said, nudging him briefly on the shoulder. "Are you high on something?"

Marco, his concentration broken, turned toward his friend.

"Marco?" Juan said again. "Are you all right?"

Marco rubbed his eyes, then said, "I'm fine."

"What in the hell are you doing out this late by yourself?"

"Just getting some air."

"It's after midnight."

"Why are *you* out so late?"

"I just left Cecilia's place. Her mother came home from her shift and chased me out."

Marco laughed. "Take your girlfriends to your place, then."

"My father won't let me have girls in my room. He's a drunk, but he holds on to his Catholicism like a damn saint."

Juan turned to glance up toward the apartment building across the street. "You're watching that old man again."

Marco nodded, the gesture lost in shadows. "All he ever does is sit at that table staring at his hands."

"Maybe he *is* crazy. But there's something else—"

Marco turned to his friend. "You think so, too."

"He's *espantoso*. I think if he stared into your face, he'd give you *el mal ojo*."

"I don't think he's evil."

"Then what is he?"

"I don't know," Marco said, turning his attention back toward the old man's window. "I wish I did know."

Juan slapped his shoulder, with force. "Leave it alone. Let the devil have him. Go home, Marco. He's trying to steal your soul."

Marco couldn't insult his friend by telling him he didn't believe in the devil or corrupted souls. He'd read too many books on science and philosophy to believe in superstitious talents, nor did the old man seem possessed of evil spirits. Something hidden lay in his behavior; he didn't know why he believed this to be true, but he did.

"Have you ever seen him on the street during the day?" Marco asked. "In a store? Walking?"

"No. I never have. Let's go, man."

"Why haven't we ever seen him during the day?"

"Let's *go*."

Marco lowered his head, thinking. Then he said, "You're right. It's getting late."

They walked away from the old man's window together, Juan ostensibly relieved he'd pulled his friend from the jaws of some infernal temptation and laughing, and Marco knowing he must return again to satisfy his curiosity. He'd spent hours studying the apartment building and the rusting fire escape hanging off its face; he only wondered if he could climb up close enough to observe the old man from the fire escape without being noticed.

* * *

The following night, Marco waited until his mother and sisters had fallen asleep before pulling on his jacket and walking down to the old man's apartment building. The street lay empty, though he still heard the echoes of strident voices in the distance; the boulevard never lost its voice, even in the deepest part of the night. He stood beneath the raised ladder of the fire escape, fingering the length of cord he'd tied to a screwdriver in his jacket pocket, waiting for the right moment to launch the screwdriver toward the last rung on the ladder. This wouldn't be the first fire escape he'd climbed in the dead of night; he knew rusting hinges often screamed out when manipulated, so he wanted to make certain he stood alone on the sidewalk before proceeding. For a moment, he questioned his presence on the boulevard, and searched for a reason to explain why he felt so strong a need to view the old man at close proximity—but no reason found its way into his consciousness.

Miraculously, the ladder only moaned softly as he pulled it down, and then he climbed up silently, like a spider, flakes of rust pressing into his palms, until he reached the third floor landing beside the old man's window. He sat on his heels for a moment, breathing evenly, glancing down on the street to ensure he wasn't being watched—then he slowly, silently, crept toward the old man's window, until his head lay against the wall alongside of it. Carefully, he turned his head so one eye could peer into the room —

Even so late into the night, the old man sat at his table, his hands before him, as if he were holding an invisible box, his eyes focused with supreme will on the air between his fingers. Marco, afraid of revealing himself, crouched uncomfortably, trying to see the old man clearly without exposing more of his face. Even through his limited vision, he noted the old man's wide forehead and thick cheekbones, his tightly curled black hair frosted with white, his large eyes cast with a pall; his skin shone like ebony, deeply, his flesh weathered but still youthful, like the stonework of an ancient temple. His hands, frozen in place, seemed large and powerful. But his face— Marco had seen pictures of people from various countries around the world, but he couldn't place the old man's heritage. He *must* have come from another country—

Then, a deep, resonant voice called out, "I know you're outside my window, son. You may as well come inside."

Marco pulled away from the window, cursing himself for letting himself be seen. He thought he'd climbed up the fire escape without a sound; he couldn't have been seen from where he'd come up from the boulevard—

"Come in. I put out a chair for you."

Reluctantly, and for reasons he didn't

understand, he turned again to gaze into the window. The old man sat with his hands in their familiar position, a wooden chair placed at the opposite end of the table. He should have fled back down the fire escape, back to his apartment—but instead, he moved forward and then climbed in through the open window. He stood staring at the old man, seeing him fully for the first time: the man's face, his entire head seemed more robust than a normal man's head, the muscle sinew of his arms visible in the lamplight, stout legs attached to a thick torso covered in a clean maroon shirt speckled with black triangles. His shining eyes stared on Marco without discernible emotion, neither angry nor welcoming. Except for the old man and the table, the only other objects in the room were a standing lamp, a neatly made single bed on an iron frame, and a large leather bag sitting at the foot of the bed.

"Sit down," the old man said, his deep voice filling the room.

Marco, his gaze fixed on the old man's shining eyes, approached the unoccupied chair carefully, and then he sat, belying his first instinct to climb back down the fire escape and melt into the shadows of the street. A compulsion held him, a *feeling*, a sense of the occasion he didn't understand but knew he must obey. He glanced at the old man's hands a moment, then back to the glassy eyes which held his full attention.

"What is your name?" the old man said.

"Marco Sanz."

"You were born in Oakland?"

"San Leandro. My mother moved us into Oakland after my father left us."

"Why did he leave?"

"I don't know. He didn't leave my mother for another woman, though. He just left."

"A boy shouldn't grow up without his father."

Marco, resenting the old man's intrusion on the subject of his father, said, "What does it matter? He's gone. So I have to grow up without my father, so the hell what?"

"The world keeps changing its traditions in ways that always sadden me."

"What's your name, then?"

"Nana."

Marco laughed. "That's a strange name. Nana what?"

"Only Nana. After the people who adopted me when I returned to the lands of my birth. They are the Nanaque. My people were related to the KhoeKhoe, but they vanished long ago. I'm the only one of my people still living."

"I don't understand. Were they killed off by someone?"

"Time killed them. Long before slave traders and profiteers. Nature killed them, and the loss of their native environment."

"You're from Africa?"

"Yes."

"Which country in Africa?"

"No country."

"You had to be born in *some* country. Or were you born on the water, like on a ship? I'm not very good at solving riddles, old man."

"The lands in which I was born had no name during that time. They've had many names since."

"Carlos was right," Marco said, sitting back in his chair. "You *are* crazy. Are you drunk right now? A lot of rummies live on this street—"

"Marco," the old man said, "focus on the space between my hands. What do you see?"

Marco, smiling briefly at the old man's odd behavior, stared down on the part of the table between the man's hands. "I only see the table. And the empty air between your fingers." He glanced up again. "What am I supposed to see, exactly?"

"All of history. Do you see it?"

Now Marco laughed, certain he was paying for the old man's entertainment. Then he stopped laughing when the thought occurred to him that the old man might be suffering some form of mental illness; and then he felt ashamed for laughing, because the old man couldn't help his condition, or appeal to the people in a city, in a country, that cared nothing for old people with mental illnesses. In that moment, he hated the city, the people, the entire world for their indifference, but he was only an impoverished Mexican boy who could do nothing to solve the world's problems.

"I should go now," Marco said.

"You're free to go," the old man said quietly, "or stay, as you choose. But if you stay and keep watching the space between my hands, I'll tell you the story of my life."

Marco felt more than certain the old man's would be a painfully sad story, but he also felt guilty for intruding on his privacy, so he swallowed his objections, nodded, and resumed focusing on the space between the old man's hands.

"I was born before the first civilizations," the old man said, his voice steady and in full command of his oratory—in fact, Marco had been surprised by his lucid conversation, a talent uncommon in alcoholics. "One hundred thousand years ago, when that part of the African continent stood lush and beautiful with grasslands and forests full of birds and beasts. I was born into my clan and hunted with my father. This was during the time before the last great Ice Age, before the changing climate turned our beautiful lands arid. Great migrations of my people moved toward better environments, though the world grew cold, and only by moving south could they avoid the ice shield slowly crushing the world to the north. Other peoples tried to endure this change of atmosphere, cousins of humanity, but none survived. Over time, I watched my immediate family die, and then the next generation of my people, and then the next—but I didn't die, I kept living, and I didn't understand why I should live and everyone I loved should die. And when my own people became strangers to me, I left my homeland and traveled the world, first following the lands below the ice sheets, then the coastlines leading on to eastern territories. Undying, I traveled back and forth across the continents as the great ice fields retreated, observing the rise of humanity from Paleolithic farmers to culturally complex societies, though no society ever survived its own self-destructive evolution."

Marco, still trying to concentrate between the old man's hands, but, of course, finding the story impossible to believe, said, "No, you *couldn't* have been alive for a hundred thousand years. Not during the Ice Age, you would have died from having an accident or by being eaten by a wolf or lion or some other prehistoric animal. The only weapons those people had to defend themselves with were bows and arrows, stones, spears. You would have died long before the first civilizations."

"You know some history, Marco," the old man said. "But you don't know all of history, or *my* history. What I've said is true. And I, too, wondered why I never seemed to have accidents, or why predacious animals never seemed to find me unaware and kill me. But one night, as I slept under the stars in the dense woods of the region now called Siberia, a great bear found me lying on the grass and approached me—I thought it would kill me, but it only sniffed at my head, and then, as if directed by a force I didn't understand, it turned from me as if stricken and fled into the trees. Then I knew no animal would ever harm me. No man may harm me, either. I've lived in cities full of murderers and thieves, mercenary soldiers, but none would approach me, all seemed repelled by a force surrounding me, but unknown to me. I believe this force also guides my steps and keeps me from encountering accidents or injury. I never sicken, and I've never needed the medicines of a doctor.

I, Gnome: Rise of a Wizard
M. R. Williamson

Not long after the birth of Yenwolk Stonesmith, came the Wizard Basil Alvis to the Stonesmith home. Now, the entire town of Cutoff knew the babe was something more than just a Gnome. As Yen grew, word traveled throughout the countryside that the wizard had sent a 'Watcher' to protect the lad. Coupled with that, and the sighting of an elusive dragon near the Stonesmith home, left no doubt that normality had indeed left the village of Cutoff.

https://www.hiraethsffh.com/product-page/i-gnome-rise-of-a-wizard-by-m-r-williamson

"I've traveled in every country, and every country that assumed those countries' places, and no one ever questioned my presence among them, or felt disturbed by my appearance. I was meant to live this long, and to walk freely among all peoples, because of that which I carry in these hands."

Marco, who'd been staring at the space between the old man's hands for a while, broke off his gaze and sat back again. "I don't see anything between your hands, Nana."

"You *must* see. That's the reason you came to me."

"I came to you because I wanted to know why the hell you were sitting at a table in your room staring at your hands all night. Now I know. Listen, you tell a great story, but all I see is an old Black man in a godforsaken neighborhood sitting at a table in a flop house staring at his delusions."

"You only believe this because you cannot see all that I hold."

"What are you holding, exactly?"

"The history of our species. That's why I've lived so long, Marco, why I've seen the rise and fall of countless civilizations, why I've had to learn hundreds of languages through the centuries in order to comprehend the peoples I observed. I carry that history in my hands."

The young man shook his head, impressed by the complexity of the old man's illusions. "Why would you need to carry human history in your hands? For what purpose?"

The old man finally moved his hands and lay his palms flat on the table. Then he sighed, deeply, sorrowfully. "I don't know. I've had thousands of years to consider my purpose, my talent, my longevity, but I can only follow my sense of purpose, my instincts, which were once finely tuned by nature. A reason exists for my carrying the history of our peoples into the future, but I'll only know that reason once it's time for it to leave my hands. I don't know if that will happen tomorrow or in ten thousand or a hundred thousand years, but I know it must happen. But I'm very old now, and very tired. I've traveled to many places in the world, many cities, many villages, and I've lived many varieties of lives, but all living things on Earth are met with death. A century ago, I knew, by an instinct deep within my body, that if I'm to die I must find my successor. I'll never find my rest until I find the next pair of hands to hold all I carry."

Marco smiled again, then sobered when he realized the implications of the old man's statement. "That's why you want me to stare between your hands?"

The old man nodded. "Once I find the one who sees all I carry, I'll let that person take it in their hands. And then I'll rest."

"I didn't see anything, so I guess it's not me."

"I traveled to this city, Marco, because I felt the presence of one who could see all that I carry. And you noticed me from the street, felt the same impulse I felt so very long ago when I first held up my hands to my eyes to witness the whole of human history. I had no one to explain this phenomenon to me, and so thousands of years passed before I finally understood I was carrying this *instrument* into a time it would be needed. Do you understand?"

"I understand what you're saying, but, I'm sorry, I don't believe a word of it."

"I know all this seems too fantastic for you to believe, but it's true."

"I should go now, Nana. It's late, and this street is dangerous after midnight."

"No one will harm you, Marco."

"I've only been alive for sixteen years, not a hundred thousand. I'm not immune to bullets or knives."

"Come back tomorrow night."

"Why?"

"If in three days you don't see all I carry in my hands, then you aren't the one. Come back tomorrow night."

"It was nice meeting you, Nana," Marco said, rising. "But I don't think I'll be coming back."

The old man inclined his head and began staring at the space between his hands again. "Come if you wish. I'll stay in this room for three more nights."

Marco, no longer possessing a reason for stealth, left through the front door of the small room, a sense of unreality pressing on his shoulders like a yoke. As he hurried down the stairs of the building, he felt his curiosity had been sufficiently satisfied and he no longer had a reason to bother the old man again. He would tell no one he'd visited the old man's room—neither Juan nor Carlos would think him anything but a fool.

* * *

He hadn't intended to return to the old man's room—but as he lay on the sofa in his family's apartment, the sounds of the street echoing up to disturb his sleep, he kept seeing the old man's face in his mind's eye, his eyes cast in a white sheen, having seen only a difficult life, or perhaps thousands of years of history—and though his logical mind told Marco to forget fantastic stories of immortality and global wandering, his subconscious mind kept stoking his curiosity to hear more of the old man's oratory—

That same night, he gently knocked on the old man's door, afraid he'd wake the man, but Nana quickly invited him in—and Marco found him sitting at the table again, his hands before him, palms up. The young man assumed his seat again across from the old man, studying the space between the man's palms for a very long time, nearly the rest of the night, but seeing nothing. While he stared, his eyes growing fatigued in the poor lighting, the old man spoke of the times he'd lived with Chinese emperors and Mongol warlords, the first Aboriginals who'd migrated in boats to the coastlines of Australia, Assyrians and Babylonians in the Near East deserts; of the time he visited Easter Island to watch the Rapa

Nui carving the massive stone faces of their ancestral gods; of the centuries he spent living among the Peloponnese city states and the ancient Romans within their republic; of the time he sailed across the Pacific ocean to live among the cultures of the New World as they razed entire jungles to erect their massive stone temples and pyramids.

When he left the old man's room early that morning, he felt disappointment weighing him down, inexplicably, because he'd never expected to see anything manifest between the old man's hands, yet feeling cheated he hadn't. The old man spoke so confidently in all he relayed to Marco, and Marco, recognizing touchstones of historical facts he'd read himself in the public library, could only wonder about the old man's education and the depth of his knowledge—he'd spoken so convincingly, but wasn't his proposed longevity impossible?

The next night, before arriving at Nana's door, Marco stood in the shadows by the burnt-out store across the street studying the old man's third floor window. Since he'd first spoken to Nana, he'd begun to sense an unexpected connection to him, a relationship he didn't understand, or, perhaps, didn't want to understand. He thought of his father, and his father's abandonment, and hoped he wasn't only trying to find a father figure in the old man. He'd felt comforted listening to Nana's deep, full voice self-assuredly recounting an impossible personal history and found himself wanting to believe—irrationally—that the old man had been telling him the truth of his experiences. But he knew, from his own example, that endless days reading books in a library could give a man endless stories to tell youthful ears. He wasn't so gullible.

Strangely, though, as he stood focusing on the old man's window, Carlos and Juan approached his position from down the sidewalk, but when they were passing right in front of him they didn't seem to see him—he hadn't been standing so far into the shadows that they couldn't see his face—they simply didn't see him, and kept walking down the boulevard. He stood considering this bizarre event for a moment, then pushed away from the wall and crossed the street.

Again, nothing materialized for him between the old man's hands, though he sat for hours that night concentrating with all his ability.

Marco finally sat back in his chair.

"I don't think I'm meant to see anything," he said, then rubbed his face with his hands.

"You'll only see something," the old man said, "when you actually *believe* you'll see something. Now, you can't bring yourself to believe."

Marco pulled his hands from his face. "That's because the things you've told me are impossible. No one could live a hundred thousand years!"

"Only I have, Marco. So only I can say if that's true."

"Well, I'm not seeing anything, so we may as well accept it."

"You still have one more night."

"What difference could that make?"

"I've had thousands of years of memories with which to live," the old man said, leaning back in his chair in an uncharacteristic pose. "But let me tell you my fondest memory."

Marco watched the old man's face, which had lost its impervious mask and now assumed a wistful smile.

"It's my oldest memory of my father," the old man said. "On the first day he brought me with him and the men of our clan on a hunt. We tracked antelope for miles, following their spoor, circling their path so we could spring up from the grass and close in on them with our spears. His face shone like black glass in the sunlight, his eyes wide, as he instructed me on the way to position my body, hold my weapon, recognize movement in the tall grasses. When we felled our antelopes, we sang and raised our spears, and I saw my father's laughing face and laughed with him, laughed with all the men of our clan. How old is human love, Marco? I know it must be much older than myself, because when I watched my father on the hunt I felt great love for the man. I loved being in the wilderness on the hunt, I loved living in the beautiful grasslands, I loved giving my mother meat from the hunt, and bones with which she'd fashion needles, hooks, and knives. This is the way human beings began, Marco, where we all began, but we let our intelligence carry us away from such beautiful ways of life into—into *this* world we know now. When I see my father's face in my memory, I only want to find myself back in those times again."

The old man, the joy of his memory leaving his face, turned his palms up again on the table, then said, "I'm not *certain* why I must carry this history into the future, but I know what it *could* be."

"What?"

"It could be that—just as we were once one people in the time of my youth, when we lived so beautifully in nature, we'll be one people again at some point in the future, when the strife and division created by people in the different places of the world focuses into one purpose, one life again. Then, in a way I don't understand, what I carry in these hands will be given away."

"If any of what you've told me is true," Marco said measuredly, "then all you carry with you is nothing but a huge burden."

"Not a burden, son. An obligation."

Marco nodded, then said, "I'll be back tomorrow night."

* * *

He didn't believe; he couldn't believe so ridiculous a story, but since Nana had only told him to come back for three days, he thought he'd humor the man. But in humoring him, Marco would only be encouraging his delusions. Still, wasn't living in so poignant a delusion a relatively innocuous way for a lonely old man to pass his time in an indifferent world? Marco had lived his own brief life staring at poverty and violence day after day, and if he couldn't see a future for himself then he certainly couldn't see a future for humanity. He wasn't too young to be cynical—the world seemed full of selfish people living only for themselves and not for a pristine future. So if Nana's delusions gave him hope for his future, who was Marco to rob him of such an ephemeral luxury?

His family seemed not to notice when he left their apartment, as if they weren't even aware he'd opened the front door and stepped out into the night. He walked down the sidewalk, distracted by thoughts which left him vulnerable to hidden threats, but no one seemed to see him either, no one met his gaze or studied him as he passed, a gesture practically a survival tactic in his neighborhood. Then he entered the old man's building and knocked on the door of his room.

Marco found Nana sitting at the small table once again; he said nothing as he sat in his own chair, uncertain of his motivations. The old man's eyes remained focused on his hands, as if he could see a spectacular collage of images lighting between his fingers.

"I don't think humanity has a future," Marco said, hoping his pessimism wouldn't upset the old man. "I've been thinking about people, and the world, and I just can't see any chance for us."

Nana sat quietly, as if he hadn't heard the young man speak. Then his glassy eyes gazed up from his hands and into Marco's face. "You only say this because you can't see all I've seen."

"What have you seen? If you've really lived for thousands of years, all you've seen is war, murder, disease, disasters. All you've seen is prejudice and slavery and genocide. I know, I've read history books, too. People are violent, angry animals. They'll only end up destroying themselves before they ever see a future worth knowing."

"Yes, I've seen wars," the old man said, "and plagues, and earthquakes, and droughts, and famine. I've seen our species behaving like animals. I've seen slavery and cruelty you couldn't even *begin* to imagine. That's why I have hope for the future. Humanity *must* live long enough to find its deliverance from its worst traits. I have faith."

"You're living alone in a cheap room. Staring at your hands all day and night. Can't you see what's happened to you?"

"Stare into the space between my hands, Marco. Please, believe. Believe you will see all I've seen. You have a gift."

Marco laughed. "I don't have any gifts."

"The place where you're born doesn't diminish the gifts you receive, son."

"This is an ugly street, old man. Haven't you seen?"

"Have you seen anything *but* these streets? I've seen thousands of streets all over the world. None could keep me from my purpose."

Marco raised his hands in surrender. "What do you want me to tell you? I can't see a *damned* thing between your hands."

"This last time, Marco. And I'll try to pass all that I hold to you. Now, place your hands on the table. Hold them open next to my hands. Look, now."

Marco sighed, then placed his hands, palms up, next to the old man's hands. Then he leaned forward in his chair to stare at the space between the old man's fingers—

As he stared into space, the minutes passing without offering any revelations, he considered his own life, the times he remembered sharing with his own father, the pain of the man's abandonment, the resentment which blossomed inside him over the years. He thought of his time surviving bad schools, the beatings he received along the way, the fights in which he engaged in a bloody adolescent ritual—he remembered the times he'd spent wasting his life with Juan and Carlos, and the endless hours he'd spent reading one book after another at the reading tables of that branch library, searching for an escape in their pages, a reason to feel hope for his future, and seeing nothing but words. After all, he was only another poor Mexican boy, just as Nana was only an indigent old Black man, surviving in a world slowly spiraling into a psychotic virtual reflection of all the selfishness, violence, and hatred which had existed long before he was born. And he simply couldn't see a future for it.

As Marco sat thinking and staring, his focus suddenly blurred, and he wondered if he was beginning to fall asleep after concentrating for so long on the empty air between the old man's hands. But he didn't feel drowsy; instead, the light seemed to brighten and dim in the room, as if the electricity were failing; he didn't want to turn his eyes away to clear his senses, knowing that if he did he would certainly give up on this final session. He forced himself to focus on the old man's hands despite the visual effects he experienced—and then, strangely, he thought he caught sight of an image in the air—a rushing of horses, of cavalry—but he wasn't high, he hadn't been drinking—then men wearing metal plates across their chests, helmets on their heads, holding swords in their hands—and then the men vanished, replaced by women dressed in woven flax moving through a thicket, bent, their hands plucking objects from the bushes they inspected; he knew they were selecting berries and placing these in woven reed baskets to be eaten in the evening when all the people in their families gathered for a holiday—

Marco watched an endless stream of images flashing to life between the old man's hands, Chinese warriors, Arab engineers, Jewish merchants in medieval markets, priests at their prayers, children running and playing in sunlight cast a thousand years ago—an endless stream of faces, clothing, demeanors, Egyptian pharaohs consulting priestesses, farmers tilling their fields, half-naked Paleolithic craftsmen flaking pieces from flint cores; he'd lost the ability to feel shocked by the visions he perceived, because as he perceived them the explanations for these images rose up in his thoughts and gave him an understanding of everything passing between the old man's hands.

Marco knew his visions were impossible—the old man must have hypnotized him in some way—but he couldn't bring himself to look away.

As if from a distance, he heard the old man's resonant voice say, "Place your hands outside of my hands now, son."

Marco obeyed, and when the old man moved his hands away the images remained, flashing and beautiful, between Marco's fingers.

He sat for hours staring at the images he held between his hands, learning the forgotten history of his species, knowing the wisdom of kings and queens, the scholarship of ancient academics, the breadth of mathematics drafted by modern physicists. He witnessed the daily lives of people moving through their native environments five hundred thousand years before, the construction of stone temples, of bridges, of cathedrals, of skyscrapers. Fascinated, he found he couldn't stare away from all he held between his hands—and he found himself believing, without any doubt, in the truth of his gift.

Eventually, Marco broke his gaze away, then stared at his open hands again, knowing he could conjure similar visions any time he wished; the knowledge seemed to come into his mind without his volition, but he knew its truth and didn't doubt this new reality. He, too, held all of human history in his hands, and would carry it with him into the future, just as the old man had done for so many years.

When he turned from the table to question Nana —endless questions had come into his mind—he found the old man lying on the single bed, his dark hands folded over his chest, his shining eyes closed on the world. Marco rose from the table and approached the bed, hoping Nana had only fallen asleep, but *knowing* that the man lay dead after so many sleepless millennia. He stood over the old man's quiet body, wishing he could say a prayer for his passing, but were there any prayers for a man who had lived for a hundred thousand years through so many spiritual manifestations? And he wondered, as he stood staring down at Nana's peaceful expression, if he would live a hundred thousand years himself before giving away all he held within his hands; or if he would give these visions to another—or if the old man's vision of a singular humanity might even become a reality one day for so fragmented and hopeless a species.

As Marco left the old man's room, he turned off the lamp, closed the door behind himself, then slipped his hands into the pockets of his jacket before returning to the shadows of the boulevard.

Close to the Wind
Gustavo Bondoni

"It's not proper for you to go to the spirits. Let them come to us." The king scowled down at them from his favorite stone, the one he liked to perch upon to receive visiting dignitaries and, apparently, also the one upon which he liked to stand when pontificating.

Mainuhpa froze, and attempted to gauge the king's mood. Though they were brothers, Olisihpa had been anointed heir to the throne because his mother was the favored wife. That was when their paths had diverged: the ruler was, as befitted his position, a man of substance. His body had grown into its glory, until, though he was still in his early twenties, his girth was that of two men. He was everything a king should be, and commanded more than enough men to overpower Mainuhpa's crew of four, if his fury was aroused.

He didn't look angry or violent, however. "I don't think they're coming to us, Olis. They have forsaken us for some reason, and if it goes on, our city will starve. We must go, as supplicants."

"Then let someone else go. You're the brother of the king."

Mainu looked down at his cordlike arms and flat stomach, tempered to a golden brown by the sun. "No one else has a chance of returning alive."

"Perhaps," Olisihpa agreed. "But it still isn't seemly."

"Will you forbid it?"

The king thought about it. "No."

Olis probably thought he'd get himself killed... which had certain political advantages, since Mainu, though not named king, was still firstborn.

"Thank you." Valhihpa, Mainu's best friend and first mate was already casting off and the two other crewmen were waiting to begin rowing. The sail would be of no use until they left the city and passed the breakers.

The stone-lined canals of Nan Madol weren't the ideal place for his large boat, two canoes linked together by a raft-like center section from which sprouted the mast, but Mainu prided himself on his ability to navigate anywhere. His crew wouldn't scrape this boat, and they wouldn't dawdle either.

People lined the waterway; rumors of his departure had been circulating among the elite of Nan Madol for days, and no one wanted to miss the actual event. Elders, men of working age, mothers and children waved to them. Young girls removed flowers from their hair and threw them down on the travelers.

Mainu relaxed and let the feel of the water flow through him, extending his thoughts only to nudge the currents when the boat needed a correction. His magic worked best when he was one with the elements.

He scanned the crowds, looking for one particular face, but the girl he wanted to see, the only flower he would make every effort to catch as if floated down from the wall, was absent. His heart sank, but he couldn't decide whether it was sadness or trepidation driving it. Kalani was utterly unpredictable.

He shook his head. Time enough to worry about that when they got back.

If they got back. The spirits made Kalani look like a paragon of stability.

Mainu nudged the water, speeding up the flow just beneath the boat. It allowed them to move a little faster, but not so fast that it would call attention to the fact that something unusual was happening. People would just assume that the boat had just caught a lucky current.

The reality, of course, was different. To move the water nearest the hull meant making the water just below that move as well... and so on. The ripples of what he did extended all the way to the bottom of the channel, and he felt every eddy as if it were part of him.

Finally the canal opened onto the sea. The waves were negligible, the wind calm, a perfect day to set out on a long voyage. They were soon past the breakers and heading out into the vast emptiness.

"Mainu," Valhihpa said, pointing, "a sail."

Sure enough, a single canoe approached. Much smaller than theirs, it was meant to be managed by a single fisherman. Canoes like it were ubiquitous around the island, crewed both by the inhabitants of Nan Madol and the people of the mainland. But only one of them had a sail.

"That little..."

Valhi's laugh cut off the rest of Mainu's phrase. He didn't want to show his true feelings in front of his friend... and he also wasn't quite certain what he would have said.

"She's catching us."

"How? There's no wind."

But, sure enough, the little boat was making ground swiftly. Kalani had probably been planning the ambush all morning, and she was perfectly positioned to intercept them. There was no way they were going to outrun her without adding hours to their journey.

"Stay on course."

She caught them a few minutes later and Mainu knew he was in for it. Her pretty, round face was creased and clouded over. He'd never seen her quite that angry.

"Were you planning on saying goodbye at any point?" Kalani asked.

"I looked for you along the walls. You weren't there."

"Of course not. I'm not some baby just off my mother's teat who is overawed at the spectacle of a boat sailing the canals. Why would I watch?"

"To say goodbye."

"I have no interest in saying goodbye."

"Then why did you follow me out here?"

"Because I'm coming with you."

"This is no place for a woman."

That didn't help matters. The anger that had been simmering just below the surface broke free. "Have you already forgotten what happened the last time you questioned me?"

Mainu hadn't. He wouldn't forget as long as he lived, and the episode was already becoming legend among the tribes. He'd tried to explain that she was smaller, that her boat was lighter, that the race hadn't been fair, but no one cared to listen. All they knew was that the former champion had been thrashed by a young girl... beaten by an entire lap of the traditional challenge course.

All Mainu knew was that she was very fast. He'd even used his magic to try to catch her... to no avail.

"I remember, but this is different. It's not just sailing. We may encounter enemies." He lowered his voice. He didn't want the crew hearing the next part, not even Valhi; his friend was a simple man, loyal but sometimes overly imaginative. "There might be monsters."

"You have to get there, first. And you won't. Not unless I'm sailing the ship."

"Out of the question."

"If you don't let me come, I'll just follow you."

"You'll die in the first big wind. Your ship isn't meant to be this far from shore."

"Then I'll die."

He looked into her eyes. She looked back, unwavering.

Mainu sighed. "I'm going to regret this."

But he helped her lash her tiny boat to their larger one.

***

The empty blue wastes stretched forever. Nan Madol and the big island, Pohnpei, were long lost beneath the horizon. The occasional fish glimmered beneath them, but other than that, they might have been the only living creatures in the universe. Even the birds were gone.

His crew seemed nervous, but Mainu wasn't worried. This had been the plan all along—no one expected their destination to be easy to reach. It would take them a number of days to arrive.

Besides, it was nearly impossible to worry when one was constantly irritated, and Kalani appeared to be determined to keep him that way.

"Have you thought about why the spirits have decided to punish the people of Nan Madol?" she asked.

"Yes, I have. It was obviously some sort of oversight on our part. The rituals we brought with us are old, perhaps some were lost on the journey, or perished in the days of my grandfather. Perhaps some wise elder died before they could pass on the wisdom."

"So the rituals have been wrong for decades, maybe even since the very first time your people landed on Pohnpei and began to build the stone channels of the city... and yet the spirits have only just reacted now?"

"They're not just my people, Kalani. They're you're people, too."

"Only on my father's side, and he died before I ever met him."

That was true. Kalani had declined every offer to live in a real room in a stone building in the city as was her right as a daughter of one of the noble cast... but she preferred to live in the heat and squalor of a thatched hut like the common race, conquered people of the island. She claimed she wanted to be by the sea, but Mainu suspected it had more to do with wanting to be far from the priests and his brother's court.

Normally, her independence delighted him. They could sit together and discuss life; even though she was much younger than he, Kalani was the only person on the entire island—noble or peasant—who cared about the sea the way he did. They could spend hours talking about that most taboo of subjects: whether there was land beyond the Outer Islands, or if the place, that distant atoll from whence Mainu's ancestors had sailed was the end of the world.

They'd speak of what might lie beyond, of how they could reach the realm of the spirits. Those long afternoon conversations had done more than just convince everyone on the island that Mainu and Kalani would soon be joined beneath the marriage arch—they'd also planted the seed in Mainu's heart that he needed to sail to the sunrise.

She'd been his inspiration. He just never imagined she'd come along for the ride.

"Can we discuss this later?"

Kalani nodded. "As you wish, but it's the kind of thing you should have clear in your mind before you confront the spirits." She stalked away, but it was difficult to go very far in the tight confines of the boat.

He sighed. At least the sea was cooperating, not that it had any choice, of course. His connection to the waves beneath him was perfect and the water had no choice but to obey his commands.

Even better, it was telling him where to go.

There is a rock. A new rock. The water doesn't know how to flow around it yet.

***

They reached the rock two days later, and everyone on board prayed for forgiveness. They would be trespassing soon.

But how soon was an open question. The rock was roughly circular, with sheer rock walls and a brutal coastline of jagged outcrops. In Mainu's world, islands were flat, welcoming places with a sandy beach to land upon. This one rose higher than the tallest trees on Pohnpei, and showed no weak spots.

Except one: a massive waterfall, like the tiny steps in the little streams that crisscrossed the mainland of their own island but on an unimaginable scale, fell like a curtain across one face of the island.

Beyond it, as the water ebbed for an instant, they could spy the mouth of a cave big enough to hold their ship, mast and all... but if they tried to sail inside, they would be crushed by the thundering water.

Valhi called over from where he was tying a rope. "It's no use. We can't land."

"Do you think we can swim over?" Mainu shot back.

"I wouldn't want to try it. Those rocks look like they could rip you up if a wave caught you wrong."

Valhi was right, but the water would do his bidding. There was no real fear for Mainu... except that he didn't think he'd be able to climb too far once he got past the shore.

Still, what choice did he have? He handed the rope he was holding to one of the crew and moved to the edge of the boat nearest the shore.

A hand on his arm gave him pause.

"No." Kalani's eyes burned into his. "This isn't the way it should be. We need to stay together."

He was about to tell her that he was the prince, and he was the only one that mattered... but that probably wouldn't go down well. As he paused to think of the right way to tell her what he was thinking, another idea occurred to him. There was another option.

But it would mean exposing his most closely kept secret, something he'd kept from everyone since childhood.

He pulled himself together and tensed to jump.

"Don't. I mean it."

The tone caught his attention. It was distant but commanding, the kind of voice that demanded to be obeyed. And there was something in her eyes. Did she know the secret he'd worked so hard to conceal, even as he used it to cheat in their race? "If you leave me here, I'll never see you again."

"Why do you say that? Don't you trust me to succeed?"

"I don't know. I just know that if you go alone, this mission will fail." The was no doubt in the words, no hesitation.

He bowed his head. He would do what it took to help his people. Only the spirits could return the balance, restore the production of the little farmland they had and make the seas bountiful again. Looking down now, he saw shoals of fish, enough to feed the entire island for months, swimming in the crystal waters beneath the boat. The fish still lived, but they were staying far from Nan Madol.

"All right." Mainu turned to Valhi. "Sail towards the waterfall. Aim at the middle and don't steer off course or we'll hit the rocks."

Valhi stared and didn't move. "Mainu..."

"He's the captain," Kalani said. "If you don't steer the ship, I will."

The wind cooperated, but Mainu hesitated to use his magic on the wall of water until the last moment. He prayed that the spirits would have mercy on him and keep him from having to reveal himself.

The spirits weren't in a merciful mood and finally, he lifted his hand and willed the curtain to part, half-afraid that it wouldn't budge, that he'd left it too long. If so, at least death would be quick. Violent, likely painful, but quick.

The water moved away, opening the cave mouth, obeying him as water had always done. He was only minor royalty on land, but ruled the sea.

Only spray remained for them to sail through, and he breathed deeply as they passed. The mist had a salty tang to it.

They sailed into the cave, the sudden silence even more oppressive than the lack of light. It wasn't just the roar of the falling water that was missing—the waterfall hadn't returned, it was as if, in parting it, he'd banished it—but also other sounds as well: the wind buffeting the sail and the cords of the ship, the gentle slap of the prow against waves tamed by his will. None of them were present, the silence was absolute.

The pool in which they sailed had no waves, there were no ripples to splash against the hull. It was perfectly round, illuminated only by the light coming in through the cave opening.

No, he corrected himself. There was more light. Light from above.

Mainu looked up to see a round circle of light. The top of the island was open to the sun.

Tales From the Quantum Café by Alan Ira Gordon

A collection of oddments created over lunch—you'll find them in this volume. There's an homage to the Thimble Theater; a treatment of the Revolutionary War in terms of a baseball game; small-town environmental problems; a random pun here and there; life on the Outback; the secret of the Drake equation; an off-beat look at Disney; and much, much more!

https://www.hiraethsffh.com/product-page/tales-from-the-quantum-cafe-by-alan-ira-gordon

In fact, the entire island was hollow, a shell of rock formed like a giant cone.

"Can anyone see a way out?" he asked. His voice echoed around the chamber, a hollow ghost of itself. The very air seemed to absorb sound.

No one replied. Valhi stared. The rest of the crew were huddled at the other end of the boat, as far as they could go without actually falling overboard. Even Kalani looked at him suspiciously.

Well, at least that answered one question: she actually hadn't known.

"Yes. I know. I can control water." He looked them over. "But somehow, I think it would be better to talk about it later."

Uncomfortable, unconvinced and unconvincing gestures of assent returned. He'd have to be satisfied with that until he could talk to them.

Wordlessly, he descended from the boat. The water was waist high and perfectly still. His eyes adjusted to the gloom and he realized that a rocky ledge ran along the shore, just a couple of hand-lengths above the water. He quickly pulled himself up.

The ledge felt perfectly dry, the stone warm against the soles of his feet.

Echoes and splashes told him that his companions had followed. He relaxed: the hardest step was past. He'd been afraid they would refuse to accompany him, would be too afraid of what they'd seen.

The ledge ascended in a spiral, and within a few moments they'd climbed the as high as several men standing on each other's shoulders. The ridge grew narrower there, and he pressed himself against the wall; a fall from that height into shallow water would break bones... or worse.

Just as he was about to call a halt because the path was too narrow to continue, he spotted a dark opening in the rock only a few paces away. Holding his breath to try to make his chest smaller, he turned sideways and advanced. Only once he was through the hole did he dare to breathe again.

Kalani was next, then the four crewmen, with Valhi at the rear, staying as far from Mainu as he could.

The gulf between them would be hard to cross... his friend held the spirits and anything related to them in awe that bordered on terror.

The passage became dark as the most overcast night. Only by keeping hands against the wall could they tell which way was forward. The air pressed in on them, cold and clammy. Mainu could almost feel the spirits brushing his skin.

Then the lights began. Fireflies lit up in the enclosure... and changed: blue and green and purple, colors that no firefly on the island had ever even imagined.

Alarmed, Mainu swatted at one of the flickers, but either it was too quick for him or he simply couldn't see them well enough to make impact.

Or, he realized as he watched one of the lights spar straight through Kalani's chest without apparent damage to either, perhaps they just weren't really there. The stuff of spirit wasn't visible to his people, but if it ever had been, he imagined that these lights were what it would look like.

The lights, the darkness, the corridor, all disappeared and he was suddenly in a place of fire. Fire all around him, but somehow in liquid form, or even solid. Solid fire.

The sense was of being deep underground, of being surrounded by rock that cut off the air to your lungs and constricted you to the point of suffocation. He tried to scream, but no sound came out... and besides, who would have heard him? His companions were long gone, lost to the liquid flame.

The whispers reached him next. Tendrils of thought, wisping at the edge of his consciousness, brushed his thoughts and left traces of themselves there. Ideas floated through him almost, but never quite, identifiable. Though alien, they were almost familiar... he'd sensed something similar somewhere.

Ah, yes. The spirits of the water. But those were placid, eager to please. They obeyed his every command with something akin to glee. These resisted any effort to communicate, brushed off all approach.

That soon became the least of his worries. Fire shot through his mind as presences probed deep, testing, questioning... evaluating. He felt that his very life hung in the balance as the process threatened to overwhelm him.

And then there was sunlight.

Mainu blinked. He was standing on a ledge on the rock, high above the sea. There was no doubt that it was the same island—the conical rock formation was unmistakable—but the passage they'd been in had disappeared. Nothing but solid rock lay behind. There was no way back inside, no chance to reach the boat.

Kalani stood behind him, followed by three members of the crew, all blinking and trying to find their bearings. Relief surged when he saw Valhi rubbing his eyes. They'd gone through a lot together, and maybe this would help the man to overcome his terror of the spirit world.

But then his stomach sank. Behind Valhi, there was no fourth man. Or rather there was, but...

The shape of a man, composed completely of rock, protruded from the hillside. One hand clutched for the sky, as if striving for freedom from his stony prison. Hs body contorted in agony and his expression was one of unimaginable pain.

Mainu shuddered and turned away. There was nothing he could have said, certainly nothing he could do. The path, spiraling along the hillside, led upward, so up they trudged, in stunned silence.

Moments later, they reached the top of the island. The monotony of grey rock was finally broken by an explosion of green. Trees, ferns, plants they'd never seen before barred their way. The path they'd been following became a mere suggestion of space between the trees.

"We're going to die here," Valhi moaned. But he kept walking, staring straight at his feet, apparently just waiting for the killing blow.

Mainu stopped and let everyone else pass. His friend reached him and, when his eyes reached the prince's feet, he shied back—Valhi knew Mainu's feet as well as he knew his face. Mainu grasped his shoulder. "Wait. Look at me."

A reluctant head straightened. Frightened eyes held his for a fleeting instant before turning away. "What?" Valhi mumbled.

"I'm the same man I always was. Nothing's changed. I don't know what you think but, to me, you're still my best friend, my only true friend.

The gaze softened, but only somewhat. "We'll see."

Mainu's two decades of friendship with the man told him that was all he would get for now, that Valhi would arrive at his own conclusions in his own time. He turned back.

The path, what there was of it, led to the center of the island. In the undergrowth, there was no real choice but to follow. Kalani led the way... Mainu suspected that trying to stop her in order to keep her safe would have been unwise.

As suddenly as it appeared, the forest ended. The center of the island opened onto a clearing of flat stone. Some sort of stone altar dominated the far end.

It was a curious construction, or perhaps a carving. It seemed to Mainu that the structure grew out of the bare rock, and spread to a flat tabular shape. Something was moving above the altar, but it was difficult to discern what it was. About ten paces from the altar, set in what looked like the exact center of the clearing, was a round hole... he supposed it was the one they'd seen from below, the source of the cavern's illumination.

They had to skirt it to approach the altar.

That's far enough.

The voice was in his head but, judging by the way Kalani and the rest jerked to a halt, they could hear it, too. It, like the whispers in the tunnel, had the unmistakable feel of the spirit world.

Mainu stepped forward. "We have come to talk, we mean no harm."

For a second the air above the altar burned with a thousand pinpoints of red glow, and the sensation—not the sound, just a sense—of amusement reached him.

You are no threat to us. But unless you can live in heat a thousand times worse than a naked flame, you would be wise to remain where you are.

Now he felt the heat, rising like a wall in front of them. Realization hit. "You're spirits of fire."

Not quite. We're spirits of the land you walk upon. Stone and fire are one, deep under the ground.

Keenly aware of the deadly drop into the shallowest of waters behind him, Mainu nodded his head in respect. "I apologize for not knowing that."

You are right to respect the spirits. So many of your kind don't. Like the man who was punished in the cavern. He didn't believe until the last moment. But then, it was too late for him. A pause and a blue glow. An encouraging glow? Mainu hoped so. *State your request.*

"We need help... the food, the food from the sea, it's gone. We're close to starving."

And what of the food from the island?

"There is none. That's what the people tell us."

Are you the king that they should tell you?

"No. My brother is the king."

Silence ensued as the lights above the altar flickered through every color imaginable and many that weren't.

He is not the king. He is a usurper, and therefore an invader. You are the king.

Mainu wanted to argue, wanted to defend the man he'd always respected as his ruler, but deep inside, he knew they were right. He'd felt the stirrings in his blood ever since he was a child, and he knew what they meant. The very waters of the island, the spirits they contained, said that Mainu was the rightful ruler.

Mainu, of course, had never listened, never acted upon it. After all, if men were satisfied to follow the brother, then Mainu was satisfied to sail on the ocean with the sun and wind caressing his skin. Why exchange his carefree life for the political intrigue of ruling Nan

Madol, the city of stone channels, and the people of the much larger island it held under its sway? No, Olisihpa was welcome to the feathered scepter that marked his office.

"Everyone accepts him as king."

Of what concern is that to us? He is not the heir, not the firstborn to whom the mantle of the spirits passed. As such, he, and his people, will starve. When we helped you to build your city, after you washed up on the shore of Pohnpei you promised to rule in harmony with the people already there, people who'd shown their devotion to the spirits for countless generations. This promise, you've ignored.

"We have done what was always done."

But not what was promised. The lights glared, nearly blinding him. Around him, his companions flinched back towards the hole and certain death. Your father ruled as a tyrant, so he was struck down in his prime... after we'd given the power to speak to the spirits of water to his successor.

"Me..."

Yes. And we also created your mate, one who can speak to the spirits of air. She is of the people of Pohnpei, and you will take her to wife when you rule. That way Nan Madol and Pohnpei will finally live in harmony with each other, and with us.

"And who speaks to the spirits of the land?"

That is not necessary, we speak for ourselves. If we want your attention, we will have it. The lights blinked. Impatiently? Now go, return to your land. Remove your brother from the throne that was never his, the throne he knows can never be his. He'll gladly give it up.

He thought of Olisihpa, menacing, on the rock. "If you believe that, you don't know my brother very well."

This time, there was no doubt. Impatience or anger, it didn't matter the glare came stronger, but now the wall of heat pushed them, almost physically, back towards the gaping opening in the ground.

Your mate will assist you. Your brother will not stand before the combined power of air and water, supported by the land itself. The combined power of your people and the islander. He will crumble without a fight, without violence. Fail, and your people will die.

Mainu reeled. He didn't want to rule, didn't want to overthrow his brother. All he wanted was to sail and fish and race Kalani...

Kalani! He would die before giving her up.

But the spirits always spoke true. Nan Madol, all of his people would die if he failed to obey. So he would have to give up the love of his life for some island woman who probably didn't even know how to clean herself in the accepted way.

Now wasn't the time to think of it, however. The burning air pushed them back towards the hole. It came from all around and made escape impossible.

Another of the crewmen, a young boy that Mainu barely knew, stumbled and fell, screaming, over the side. Mainu chanced a glance down to see the broken body far below, the water around it dark with blood.

Then he was gone, too. The burning air forced him to take that final step into the abyss and he dropped, surrounded by his companions.

The air rushed by and Mainu closed his eyes and waited for the impact that would tear the life from his body, dead among his beloved spirits of water.

The impact never came. After some moments, he opened his eyes to realize that his three companions were suspended motionless in the air the height of a tall man above the water. Air rushed past, pushing him, keeping him from falling, tearing at his hair, his loin covering, his beads.

Then the wind stopped and they fell, to land sputtering but unhurt in the shallow pool.

No one stopped to question their fortune. They rushed to the boat and sailed it through the opening, Valhi pausing only long enough to pick up the shattered boy.

Only when they were out in the open sea did anyone speak.

"The spirits of the air saved us," Mainu said.

"Yes," Kalani replied, looking away as she said it.
"But the spirits do not act on their own."
"Perhaps they did," she replied.
"Did they?"
Kalani said nothing.

Mainu smiled. Suddenly, despite the tragedy of two deaths, and the fact that he would need to betray his brother, his burden seemed bearable, his choice possible.

"You controlled the spirits. You saved us."

Kalani said nothing.

"I don't need you to answer. I know the truth already."

She looked out into the distance, jaw set firmly, eyes hard.

Mainu let the silence stretch on. He knew just how hard it must be for her to have her most closely held secret revealed in that way. He smiled. Served her right for not telling him.

"Will you be my queen?"

She looked up and something in his face must have convinced her that he was sincere because tears welled in her dark eyes. It took a while before she managed to force the words out. "Of course. I would have been your queen even if you hadn't been a king."

They sat in silence, the water and the air collaborating to push their little boat across the water at a velocity he'd never experienced before. Sails billowed out like the stomach of a senior courtier, but the boat wasn't buffeted—every gust was transformed into pure speed.

A thought hit him and he stood and faced Kalani.

"The race! You cheated. You used the air to—"

He never completed the sentence. A sudden gust pushed him overboard; the waiting water caressed him.

As Valhi pulled him aboard, Mainu realized the message the wind had given him. It was time to set childish things like the race aside. He and Kalani had acted like children too long. It was time for them to combine their powers for the good of their people.

The time for competing against each other was past.

Trixie
K. S. Hardy

I guess the first sign that something was there, was the slippers.

Returning home from the office supply store where I was taking advantage of their back-to-school month-long sale to stock up on cheap notebooks and pens because I do heed King's advice that computers and typewriters can fail you when the creative flow is full on, I discovered upon opening my side door a pair of cinnamon-colored cloth slippers awaiting me.

What was odd about that, one would ask?

The slippers were a gift from someone, not my wife, so long ago I no longer remember who gave them to me. And since I live in southern California where the weather is almost constantly warm, it is my habit to barefoot it around the house and sometimes outside. Said slippers I thought had been exiled to the back of some graveyard of a closet or dumped in one of those charity bins found in parking lots.

Also I was home alone.

Constance was off to New York on one of her Broadway orgies with some of her friends where they tried to see as many plays as possible in a week. And since I was not too obsessed with what the place looked like, the housekeepr had the week off also.

So where did the slippers come from?

I kicked them aside. Set my bags on the kitchen counter. And then with a sense of wariness, explored the rest of the house. Nothing jumped out at me like a cat in a cliché-filled horror movie. Nor did I find a robber or bogeyman creeping about the hallways.

The house was empty.

The slipper incident was filed away in my mind as something to be pondered later, as I had a novel that was waiting, and the deadline was approaching. Even though I am considered a successful writer (New York Times Best Seller list, although I find it a miracle that I make the list) and could comfortably live off the royalties already accrued, I feel the most desperate need to feed the publishing machine. Besides, the book I was working on was getting extremely interesting and although I already knew how it was going to end, I was so excited that I wrote well into the night.

The second sign came the next morning. Or should I say, was delivered.

I had slept in, which is not hard to do when your chosen career means you do not have to keep office hours. After my usual routine in the master bath I strolled down the upstairs hall with the thought of going down to poke around the kitchen in search of breakfast. I came to the door of the guest room.

It was open.

Now, the latch on this door never worked properly and the slightest pressure could cause it to open—a problem I had always intended to have fixed but never seriously enough to get around to it. I often write of a sense of unease or trying to stimulate that same sense in the reader, but I can tell you, at that moment, I was feeling it myself. For if the latch had released by itself—for example, if it was tripped by a twitch of the nearby San Andreas fault, the gap resulting between the jamb and the door edge would have been only an inch or two.

But the door was ajar by almost two feet. An earthquake causing a gap that size would have awakened me. No, someone or something had opened the door wide enough to slip inside.

Cautiously I peered into the room, changing my position bit by bit so I could view as much of the interior of the room as possible. It appeared unoccupied. Standing to the right of the hinged side so as to be shielded by the wall, with the flat of my palm I eased the door completely open. Nothing happened. No hungry tiger escaped from the circus leaped out at me. I looked into the room again with now a wider perspective. Empty. As empty as the house was the night before.

I stepped inside. And I saw it.

At the foot of the bed on the floor lay a quilt my wife had bought at an art fair some years previously. It was rumpled and crumpled into a little next. No longer folded over the bedstead's foot board in display.

Trixie.

Trixie was the one who regularly would pull the quilt down and leave it arranged in such a manner.

Trixie had come home.

Of course I was unnerved. Either someone was playing an elaborate joke on me, something my friend Richard might conceive of, but he had sadly passed over some years before, or I had acquired a ghost.

I got no work done that day. Instead I went to a new bookstore that had opened recently in a city nearby and unannounced, I signed every copy of my books they had on the shelves, hoping that the good karma would follow me home.

That night in the twilight of the mind just before total sleep, I heard Trixie come up the stairs. Instantly awake, I sat up. I recognized her pace on the hardwood steps. Years and years before she left us she had come up the stairs the same way, even when she was so old the climb became difficult. It was her way of making sure we were home. Of making sure we were safe.

I could hear her panting outside my closed door.

I did not move from the bed. And I did not sleep that night.

Dawn came. I got up and with some trepidation opened the door.

She was not there.

I had thought correctly that the new day might dissuade her lingering presence. Something in the back of my memory from some research I had done for a subject suggested it. Something English, perhaps. New day, ghost away.

However, I did give the house another search.

Other than a depression in the cushions of the couch, a place where Trixie often liked to sleep without permission, everything seemed to be normal.

I went into my office/den to call my wife. It would be three hours later in New York, approaching ten in the morning, and with luck I would catch her on her cell before she got to busy.

I had not gotten past the area code when Trixie's ball rolled into the room.

The automated voice on the phone said, "Your number cannot be completed as dialed. Please try again," as I stared at it.

I ended the call.

"Please try again." Okay. I went to the ball and with my toe nudged it back into the hall.

The ball rolled back into the room. Now I knew what Trixie wanted. I looked out into the hall.

Nobody there.

I picked up the ball and tossed it down the hall out of sight into the living room. Within seconds it rolled back into the hall, bounced off the baseboard, and came toward me. I picked it up and would have thrown it again, but I sensed the game was over.

Trixie was gone.

Two days later my wife came home. I didn't even give her a chance to regale me with trip stories or show me all the stuff she had bought.

"I had a visitor while you were gone."

"Who?" she asked.

"Trixie came home."

She stopped in her tracks. "That's not funny."

"I'm not trying to be."

"This isn't a new idea you're working on?"

"No. For real, she was here."

I outlined for her event by event what had transpired.

"So you are saying our house is haunted by a ghost dog?"

"No, she's gone, now."

I could tell by the look on her face that she needed more.

"And I don't think she was here to haunt us," I explained. "I think she came back to tell us she was happy where she is now, and that everything will be okay. We don't have to worry, there is an afterwards. And she's there, wagging her tail and waiting for us."

Tears welled in her eyes. Hugging her, I wept with her. One day, Trixie would be home again.

From the mind of K. S. Hardy . . .

The tales of K. S. Hardy blend Grimm and Poe in a heady mix of dark and strange. From "Sometimes Above the Trees" to "The Snake's Defense," and all points in between, Hardy takes you on a tour through the unexpected and the inexplicable. Have a seat, put your feet up . . . and leave all the lights on.

https://www.hiraethsffh.com/product-page/weaving-the-light-by-k-s-hardy

Tin Can
Debby Feo

RR273 was not happy. Someone was repeatedly stealing some of his spare parts, particularly his Walking Legs, while he was out on the Surface of Enceladus wearing his Cruiser Rollers. RR273's Cruiser Rollers were much too large to fit into a regular Surface Elevator to get to and from the exterior of Enceladus; so he had to wear his Walking Legs to use one of the Surface Elevators. RR273's multiple storage lockers (near the top and bottom of the Main Surface Elevator), where he stored extra Walking Legs and Cruiser Rollers, were continually broken into. RR273's supply of extra Legs from Earth was dwindling fast.

RR273 was a Mid-level robot, a step above a Standard, and a step below a Sentient (aka an Android). His original use was to build, and make repairs to, equipment located on the surface of Enceladus. After the colonies on Enceladus were well laid out, both above and below the icy crust, he was fitted with Walking Legs, so that he could also be of use underground.

Periodically, RR273 was ordered down to the reinforced Residence Level, which was located above the subsurface Ziton Ocean. After the robot had finished his assigned tasks, he would return to the Surface, to the Robot Storage/Charging Center, and plug himself in, until he was needed again.

Most robots remaining on Enceladus were Standards. Standards had neither individual personalities nor discretionary abilities. Standards, for the most part, did the jobs that Biologicals did not want to do. For example, Standards had been used to dig out the shafts for all the Surface Elevators located around Enceladus. Standards were also: trash collectors, clean-up crews, servers, transporters, motion detectors, radiation detectors, ice-depth checkers, cavern checkers, etc.

Mid-level robots on Enceladus, like RR273, had some decision-making capabilities, as they were often out, all alone, on the very cold (-324°F at noon) surface. Unlike Biologicals (who were mostly Human, on Enceladus), robots did not have to breathe or protect themselves from weather extremes, with the exception that the earliest robots occasionally rusted. All newer robots were made from non-rusting materials; and Sentients, of course, had waterproof Flexiskin. (Of course, a meteorite, even a small one could destroy a robot.)

There were very few Sentients left on Enceladus. Most had been sent on to the other moons of Saturn - to help new Colonists, or to supervise groups of Standards. With the introduction of Flexiskin and the inclusion of emotions, reasoning, and deduction into their advanced programming and learning capabilities, it was becoming increasingly difficult to tell Sentients from Biologicals. With the passage of local Fair Disclosure Laws, Sentients remaining on Enceladus had been forced, in several of the colonies on Enceladus, to wear identifying nametags, with "MB" (Mechanical Being) following their chosen names.

It was not easy for RR273 to replace his stolen Walking Legs; as usual, Biologicals generally got priority on replacement parts. Walking Legs were a specialized item, thus were very expensive. This made Walking Legs a great bargaining/barter tool - which is why they were sometimes stolen. (Some "Collectors" did not ask questions as to the origin of items.)

Walking Legs could fit either robots like RR273, or some biological amputees - those who had universal connectors for their prosthetic parts.

In the beginning of the colonization of Enceladus, accidents were more likely to occur. A spacesuit might be torn during construction of Surface Domes and other buildings; or torn when someone fell thru the thinner icy crust near the four major sulci (aka the "Tiger Stripes"), at the southern pole of Enceladus. Extremities were the first biological body parts to: be frostbitten, become gangrenous, and later need to be amputated. Even in the slightly warmer underground caverns of Enceladus, spacesuits could be breached. Only in climate-controlled domes or enclosed subsurface areas could most Colonists risk removing their protective spacesuits.

For all dangerous, and repetitive tasks, robots quickly replaced Humans, the first colonists on Enceladus. However, there came a point when everyday life became less dangerous; and Humans began to question the need for robots, particularly ones that used up Human supplies.

Because of rising resentment towards robots, RR273 often met resistance at Colony Supplies stores, when he tried to shop for replacement parts.

"Robot, we have nothing for the likes of you," said the man behind the service counter.

"According to your inventory, you have the Walking Legs that I need," RR273 responded.

"You're a useless piece of metal! Maybe in the beginning Humans needed you, but not now."

"May I please speak to the manager?" RR273 asked politely.

"I am the manager. I am also the owner. Get out of here, you Tin Can!"

Not wanting to cause undue stress to a Human, the robot turned around and left Colony Supplies 14A, the latest store in which he had tried to find replacement Walking Legs.

RR273 had Walking Legs on back-order from Earth, but the shipping date was continually pushed later and later, despite his "payment" (Robots of Mid-level and above were awarded credits to use for their own maintenance.) of extra so-called "non-essential" shipping fees.

RR273 was out-of-date, as far as robots were concerned. He was certainly Not worth the money it would cost (in fuel) to transport him to somewhere that he would be more useful, and definitely *not* back to Earth. RR273, since he obeyed orders and had never harmed a Human, did not deserve to be sent to Titan's RCRR (Reprogramming Center for Rogue Robots). There was a slight possibility of the robot being sent to the Titan Robot Factory, to be "taught" different skills; but the TRF was not a big facility, thus there was a waitlist.

RR273 could have used the much larger Equipment Elevators of UGD16 (the underground colony he had been assigned to), without removing his Cruiser Rollers; but that required a Permit, which meant convincing a Human bureaucrat. RR273 was increasingly avoiding unnecessary Human contact, as he did not like experiencing enmity towards robots.

Soon, when his supply of Legs ran out, the robot would either be "stuck" above or below ground, unless he managed to "sneak" into an Equipment Elevator. He wanted to be ready for just such an emergency, so he began investigating the schedules for the two Equipment Elevators nearest UGD16.

RR273 carefully planned his surface outings and kept a "close eye" on his electrically charged batteries. Robot charging stations on the Surface had been reduced in number to save on overall expenses and were therefore only located near Surface and Equipment elevators.

RR273 doubted that anyone would come looking for him, should he run out of energy and be stranded out on the Surface of Enceladus. He would just be written off, as "defective machinery", and his personal Surface Charging Port (and storage lockers) would be assigned to a more recent model of robot.

One day, RR273 decided that he would hide near his Surface storage locker - hopefully to spot and then report, whoever was stealing from him. He had decided that he would make his report directly to the Saturn Bureau of Robotic Matters (SBRM), bypassing the local Human authorities. The robot doubted that the local Humans would even pass on any reports that he made; and certainly, would not punish the boys he suspected of stealing from him.

RR273's previous attempts to record burglaries had been thwarted by the continued disabling of the cameras that he had installed on his storage units. He had been able to repair most of the cameras, but the thieves were becoming more and more destructive. Although he had asked the local authorities for permission to review their zoned videos, he was denied access to them.

After depositing a new set of Walking Legs into his Surface storage locker, and switching into Cruiser Rollers, RR273 hid near his locker. He didn't have to wait long.

"It's gone," a boy wearing a blue spacesuit said to another boy in a green one.

"All right! I can use some extra money to make a hop to Tethys," said the one in the green suit. "I'll take care of that camera."

The boy in the blue spacesuit took out an electronic lock picker and opened up RR273's storage locker. "There's just one pair of Legs in here."

"Well, we'll have to split whatever we get for the pair."

"Almost not worth it," the boy in the blue suit said.

"It is worth it, although the more often we do this, the more chance there is that we'll get caught."

"Hey, if that robot catches us, just start to cry. He'll back off tout de suite."

"If one of the local guys sees us, I assume they'll just look away. I know my dad would. He really hates robots. He says robots take jobs away from Humans."

"I don't like robots because they think they know everything," said the boy in the blue suit.

"They may know a lot, but they're certainly not perfect!"

"Well, at least most of our robots look like robots. I hear some of those new Sentients look too much like regular Humans. Disgusting, if you ask me!"

"What does your dad think about the new Jovian Ambassador?" The boy in the green suit asked, out of curiosity.

"He doesn't like other Biologicals either. He thinks that Only Humans should be able to live on Enceladus. He'd like everyone else to be sent back to where they came from."

"Sounds like my dad," the boy in the green suit said. "But mine doesn't mind having Standards around to do the "dirty" jobs."

After the two boys had left the storage locker, each one carrying one of his Walker Legs, RR273 rolled in front of them.

"Excuse me, sirs, where are you going with my Walker Legs?" he asked.

"Run!" The boy in the blue suit said, via his intercom.

Both boys ran, but RR273 could roll faster. After he had cornered the two boys, he stretched out his robot arms around them, to keep them from escaping. The robot had already sent a distress message to the local police station; and he had requested a Human officer to respond.

"Let us go!" The boy in the green suit ordered, turning on his exterior sound.

"Not until the Police arrive," RR273 responded.

"You're hurting us," the boy in the blue suit claimed, while squeezing out some fake tears.

"I am not even touching you. I am being quite careful about that," said RR273. "I hear them, the Police are coming."

Once the police - a Human officer and two policebots - arrived, RR273 explained what had happened. He pointed out to the Human officer where he had engraved his name onto each of the Walking Legs, and showed the officer a video, on his chest screen, that he had recorded of the break-in. The two boys were arrested and taken to the nearest station by police hovercraft.

At the police station, after all the evidence was reviewed by the Police Chief and a Sentient Detective, the two boys were charged with burglary, with the sentence to be decided by a visiting Judge.

RR273, although he eventually got his Walking Legs back, and was reimbursed for the other stolen pairs (via the boys' parents), suddenly became Robot non grata. Both of his storage lockers were taken away from him, while he was out on the Surface. When he tried to approach an Equipment Elevator, alarms went off. Several local Humans surrounded him and damaged his charging port.

"What are you doing?" RR273 asked, unable to stop the men because of the hard-wired Asimov Laws of Robotics.

"Robot, you're making trouble. Get out of here!"

"Head that-a-way," an obvious Old-Timer pointed, away from the Surface structures.

So, the robot headed that-a-way, for a short distance.

"Keep going and don't stop," said the Old-Timer.

RR273 kept going, until his power ran out, unfortunately, nowhere near a Charging Station. Fortunately, before his battery ran out, he had sent out a distress signal to the SBRM, which was located on Ring C22 of Saturn. Eventually, he was rescued by local Standards.

It did not take long before Mr. Tyler, the Chief Roboticist at the Titan Robot Factory, heard about RR273's story on the Vidcom, which Mr. Tyler had programmed to alert himself regarding any news involving robots.

Mr. Tyler, who was from Ceres 2, and had the indigenous wings, had experienced being an outcast, having lived on Earth for some time, before taking a position on Titan; thus Mr. Tyler was able to empathize with RR273, even if the robot wasn't a Biological. He wanted to help any robot that got into trouble and ended up in a news story.

Mr. Tyler offered to buy out RR273's Work Contract, regardless of his condition. Then, he paid for the relocation of the robot to Titan. At the TRF, the robot would be updated , both mechanically and programming-wise.

RR273 was very grateful to Mr. Tyler. The robot never expected to be given another chance at life. He had always known that he would eventually be designated out-of-date. Then, he would be sent to a recycling plant. Thanks to Mr. Tyler, RR273 had the prospect of being valuable again.

The Protocol (A Thyme Amaretto Kill)
By Tyree Campbell (Hiraeth Books)
Review By Alan Ira Gordon

The Protocol is the first installment by author Tyree Campbell in his "Thyme Amaretto Kill" series. The setting is present-day Washington, D.C. While the city's name is never stated, from its geographic location and description of various locations within the city, it's clearly our nation's capitol, albeit with a mix of dystopian elements and echoes of our real world. The title character of Thyme Amaretto is a contract killer hitwoman who works for a shadowy federal government agency only known as The Protocol. The twist is that in this deteriorating society, contract killing is legal and Amaretto is the best of the legal hitman/hitwoman bunch.

The plot begins with a focus on City Police Detective Kallia Gibson, who is investigating various sudden appearances of pools of blood in public locations throughout the city. She soon comes into unintended contact with Amaretto, which triggers a cascade of simultaneous and interconnected events. The first result is the shadowy higher-ups in The Protocol feeling threatened by the situation and thereby putting out a hit on Amaretto. Competing hitmen take-up the challenge of killing Amaretto for the notoriety of knocking-off the best legal hitwoman in the business.

The novel's plot is layered with suspenseful cat-and-mouse scenes as the thrown-together-by-events duo of Kallia and Thyme struggle to evade an ever-tightening noose of pursuers. Tension is relieved by timely action as the duo work to save themselves while simultaneously working to solve mystery elements regarding the nature and identity of the upper echelon players of The Protocol. And as if this danger isn't enough, midway through the plot a sub-plot emerges of an immediate, massive and deadly terrorism threat which our duo must prevent on a parallel track with their fight to stay alive.

There are several elements to this novel that result in an absorbing, well-written and entertaining read. First-off is the multiple-genre issue. The foundation of the storyline is action-adventure-thriller. But right from Chapter 1, author Campbell weaves-in basic science fiction, fantasy and magical realism elements. I really don't want to provide any specific plot spoilers to illustrate, suffice to say that Thyme has magical abilities and that alien elements are built into Thyme's personal backstory as well as operating in the present-day of the plot.

Secondly, there's a subtlety here regarding the science fiction and magical elements that's intriguing. Author Campbell never brings these elements to the forefront of this first novel in the Thyme Amaretto Kill series. Instead, we see tantalizing and very small glimpses of sci-fi, aliens, magic in practice here and there in the story, serving a tidbit clues to the bigger picture of what's going-on with the main adventure thriller plot elements. This storytelling approach works very well to entertain the reader as well as whet the reader's appetite toward wanting to read future installments of the series.

Third, I was very impressed with Campbell's inclusion of a wide-ranging number of additional story characters. He skillfully fleshes out a large number of players including Protocol figures, city police force members, street urchins, hitmen and local media folk: the list goes on and on. Kudos to Campbell for taking the storytelling time and having the writing skill to make this work. Not to be overly dramatic or to take literary pretensions, but as this large cast of players take their turn center stage throughout this action-adventure, I was reminded of Charles Dicken's similar skill in unveiling an operatic cast of players within his novels (*A Tale Of Two Cities* comes immediately to mind).

And finally, perhaps most importantly as well as most entertainingly, there's the relationship between Thyme and Kallia. Unintentionally thrown-together by thriller story events, there's an initial hint of personal attraction that evolves into a full-blown eroticism between the two. And then, their personal relationship takes a very unexpected and somewhat shocking turn in the final scene of the novel. Again, I don't want to provide any spoilers here. But I will say hats-off to Campbell for providing a unique and unexpected turn in the duo's personal relationship. I sure didn't see it coming at all, and actually re-read it three times late in the evening of finishing the book's read, it stunned me that much. It's beautifully written, heartbreaking and serves as a wonderful and worthwhile bridge to the next novel in this book series that Campbell is scheduled to pen.

Tyree Campbell himself refers to this novel as something a little different from his usual novel's plotlines. And I agree. This is a very well-written and engrossing genre-related thriller that's well-worth the read, both in-and-of-itself and as something different from the author's usual science fiction storytelling approach. So get yourself a copy of The Protocol and enjoy!

The Protocol

https://www.hiraethsffh.com/product-page/the-protocol-a-thyme-amaretto-kill-by-tyree-campbell

Love After Death
Paul Lonardo

Alecia wandered the hallways of Mount Hope High School, mechanically following the routine of her regular Monday class schedule, her body trapped behind her desk while her mind wandered, lost in the darkness inside her head. The fragments of words and sentences from her classmates and teachers barely registered, while the droning bells alerted her to move on to the next class. That first day back was even worse than she'd expected. Whenever she approached a group of students of any size, their conversations instantly stopped. Everyone would stare at her, but no one said a word, not even Beth Cook, her best friend and co-captain of the cheerleading squad. One time she went into the wrong room and sat down. Twice she found herself crying. Then, near the end of the last period, her dead boyfriend blew in her ear. She had closed her eyes for a moment in English Lit when a light breeze disturbed the air around her head and she caught the scents jasmine, musk, and sandalwood, the fragrance of a cologne that she had given Braden on his last birthday.

"Alecia."

His voice was delicate as gossamer. She craved his touch. She would have given anything to be in his secure embrace once more. His hot breath tickled her neck, and she smiled. When he blew in her ear again, she couldn't take it anymore. The slow, concentrated exhalation from his lungs directly into her ear was something Braden always did when he wanted to seduce her. He knew it drove her crazy.

"Oh, Braden." There were several gasps, and when Alecia opened her eyes, everyone was looking at her, including Mr. Gablinske, the principal. He stood over her, the usual stern, authoritative cast to his face softened, his green eyes radiating sensitivity. Her streaming tears could have easily been assumed to be anguish and sorrow, but they were actually tears of embarrassment. Alecia's cheeks were flushed as Mr. Gablinske helped her to her feet and escorted her to his office, where she took a seat in front of his desk.

"I phoned your mom," he said. "She's on her way here."

Alecia nodded without looking at him.

"Maybe it's too soon," he began. He shook his head grimly and sighed. "Braden's death was a shock to the entire school. He was such a remarkable student and athlete. The best quarterback we've ever had here. As class president, he was a leader off the field as well. But I don't have to tell you how special he was."

Alecia hardly heard a word the principal was saying. Instead, her attention was focused on the football field outside the office window. The football team was gathered in the near end zone, but the players weren't stretching, running drills or doing anything to get ready for the county championship game. They were in their school clothes and standing in a circle around Coach Colletti.

"I also spoke with the school counselor," Mr. Gablinske continued. "She thinks you might need some help dealing with your loss, and believes it would benefit you to speak with a psychologist who specializes in grief therapy. She can recommend several to you and your mom."

Alecia immediately recognized Riley, who was tallest of all the boys, standing directly in front of the coach.

"Miss Soares." The principal waited for her to look up at him, but she did not. "Miss Soares. Are you listening?"

Her eyes locked on a familiar silhouette moving around behind the players. She knew the physique quite well, the broad shoulders and narrow waist, and the tangle of brown hair. Though his back was to her, she recognized the butt in the dark blue shorts with gold piping, the Mounties' school colors. A chill ran the length of her spine, making the tiny hairs on her arms stand up.

It was Braden.

He slowly walked around the other boys, but none of them reacted to him.

It couldn't be him, she thought. It was just her imagination playing tricks on her. She was unable to take her eyes off him as made his way around the group, stopping beside Riley.

Suddenly Braden looked up, turning his head in her direction and gazing directly at her.

"Alecia."

A light touch on her neck made her jump. She turned quickly and gasped when she saw her mother standing there.

"Alecia, are you okay?" he mother asked.

"He's here," she shouted as she rushed to the window. "It's him! He's here! It's Braden!"

Her mother gave Mr. Gablinske an embarrassed sidelong glance.

Alecia pressed her hands desperately against the glass. She scanned the group of boys, but Braden was not among them now. "He's gone," she said, crestfallen.

That was how Alecia's first day back at school after Braden's funeral had gone, and that was when things really started to get weird.

***

That night, Alecia was physically and emotionally exhausted, but she was unable to sleep, which was something she had gotten used to over the past week and a half. It was late when her phone rang. For a moment, she entertained the impossible that it might be Braden, who often called her at such an hour. She answered it, mumbling a hello.

"Hi, Alecia. It's Riley? Did I call at a bad time?"

"No. I can't sleep anyway."

"Good. I mean, I'm glad you're awake." Riley forced a cough to clear his throat. "I just wanted to talk to you for a minute."

Alecia picked up on something different in the way Riley spoke, a hesitancy and a restless anxiety in his tone. His voice had a vulnerable quality, and Alecia couldn't help being drawn to him. She knew she shouldn't be thinking about Riley in that way, but she couldn't help it. He was Braden's best friend, after all. Not to mention he was dating Beth.

"Sure," Alecia said cheerily, inviting further dialogue.

After a lengthy pause, Riley said, "Everything is all right, then?" His voice quavered. "I'm sorry, Alecia. That was a dumb of me to say."

"No, it's not."

"Yes, it is. It's all my fault anyway. I should have stayed and driven home with him. He would be alive today."

"You don't know that, Riley. You might have been killed along with him."

Riley sighed deeply, not knowing how to defend his failure to stay with Braden and drive him with him that night. In the silence that followed, Alecia recalled the horrific events of that night as they came to be known. Braden had been working out extra late with his offensive unit through a steady drizzle, in preparation for the 5A division championship game against Centerdale High. It was raining heavily by the time the others left, but Braden stayed behind by himself to do some drop back and foot work drills. Riley, the team's number-one receiver and backup quarterback, tried to talk him out of it, telling him that he should call it a night. But that was how determined Braden was when he had his mind set on something. It was after 10:00 p.m. when he left the field. He was taking the highway off-ramp a half mile from his house when his jeep hydroplaned off the road and into a ravine. His seat belt and air bags offered him some protection, but the jeep overturned, rolling over several times. Braden sustained serious internal injuries and was unconscious when rescue workers arrived. Efforts to save him failed, and he was pronounced dead at the hospital.

"Neither of us is the same anymore," Alecia finally said. "It's obvious I'm struggling to keep it together. I'm barely able to get out of bed in the morning, and I haven't been able to focus on anything. Now I'm starting to see Braden and my mom wants me to see a shrink."

"Wait, what did you say?"

"My mom wants me to see a shrink," she repeated.

"No, about Braden. You said you saw him."

"Well, I thought I did. He was walking around next to you and the other players this afternoon when the coach was talking to the team."

"That's funny," Riley said, exhaling sharply. "I felt him. Sort of. I think. I mean, not literally. When we were having the vote about whether or not to play the championship game, the count was always one more than the number of players there. Even when the coach counted. It was weird. It made me think that Braden was somehow putting in a vote to play."

"Is the team really considering forfeiting the game Friday?"

"Well, we're kind of split on that. I decided not to play. I don't feel right about quarterbacking the team. My heart's just not in it. I don't want the team to forfeit, but I can't do it, and the coach doesn't think we have any real chance going with Tyler or anyone else at quarterback. So, yeah, we'll probably end up forfeiting."

"I can understand that," Alecia said. "Thank you."

"For what?"

"For explaining your decision not to play in the game. That's the reason you called, isn't it?"

Riley hesitated.

"Sure, that, and I also wanted to be sure you're all right. I heard about what happened at school today. I just wanted you to know that if you ever need anything, or if you want someone to talk to, you know you can call me."

"You can call me, too," she said. That sounded stupid, she thought, since he just had called her. "It's good to know you're there," she added. "I could use a friend right now. You might be the only one I have. Everyone at school probably thinks I'm crazy, and I'm starting to think they're right."

"You're not crazy, Alecia. You're wonderful. Someday, sooner than you think, things will get better. You deserve to be happy."

Alecia sensed Riley's smile radiating to her as a wave of energy through her phone. "I am now." She wanted to say something more direct, but she wasn't sure it would be appropriate.

"I'll call you again soon to check on you," Riley said.

"I'd like that," Alecia told him.

The conversation had come to an end, but neither wanted to be the first one to say goodbye. The protracted silence that followed wasn't altogether uncomfortable, at least for Alecia.

"Okay, then," Riley stammered. "I guess I'll talk to you later. Bye, Alecia."

"Good night." She held the phone to her ear and waited for Riley to disconnect. When she glanced at the screen, she was surprised to see they had been talking for twenty minutes. It occurred to her that they'd never had a one-on-one conversation that lasted anywhere near that long before. Braden, Beth, or both, had usually been around. Alecia's cheeks were flushed, and her heart beat a quick, steady rhythm in her chest. She had a wide grin on her face for the first time since Braden died. She felt a pang of guilt for the thoughts she'd been having about Riley. Braden's presence was everywhere. Pictures of him were all around her room. The residue of their relationship wasn't just physical. He was in her heart and mind as well. She thought about him all the time. Dreaming about him was one thing, but these hauntingly realistic hallucinations were a clear indication that she wasn't over him and she wasn't ready to move on. That's why she knew that, even though she hadn't done anything wrong, she shouldn't be flirting with Riley. It would only lead him on because a relationship between them wasn't possible. Getting involved with Riley would only stir feelings of betrayal that would be too much for her to bear. She had to think of Beth, as well. She couldn't get involved with Braden's best friend, her best friend's boyfriend. It wasn't right. The next time he called, she would tell him that directly so there would be no misunderstandings and no chance of either of them pursuing something that would never happen, should never happen.

***

"*Alecia.*"

Her name had come out of Braden's mouth countless times before in so many different inflections. This time, he spoke her name tentatively, almost warily. It had been about ten minutes since she'd gotten off the phone with Riley as she laid awake streaming some music on her phone.

"*Alecia.*"

She raised her head and her eyes instantly widened when she saw him. She lifted herself upright on the bed and found herself gazing directly at Braden, who was standing in the middle of the room. She couldn't believe what she was seeing. She didn't know if she was awake or asleep at first. If she were dreaming, it was the most realistic dream she'd ever had. Alecia had never seen a ghost before, but she would have expected one to have physical qualities that were vastly different from those of the living. This was Braden, in solid human form, not an ethereal manifestation or translucent likeness. He wasn't floating in the air, his orange Nikes were planted firmly on the wood floor of her bedroom. She realized that she was looking at a ghost because Braden was dead. She had seen his body in the casket, watched them close the lid the final time and then lower the vessel into the ground. These visuals were burned into her mind, and even though she had observed them through tears and the fog of a terrible trauma, she knew they were real, and that the vision she was seeing now could not be trusted.

"Alecia." He was peering urgently at her.

"Braden?"

His eyes opened wide and his cheeks dimpled as he smiled with elation. "You can see me?"

Alecia shot to her feet and she almost stumbled. "Is it really you?" she asked, standing just a few feet from Braden.

"It's me," he said with a grin.

Alecia took a half step closer to him and extended her hand. Braden reached out, and just as their fingers touched, a brilliant pulse of blue light flared around them. It dissipated only when Alecia lowered her hand. She took a step back and gaped at Braden, who looked as stunned as she felt.

"This is impossible," Alecia said.

"You're the only person who has been able to see me," Braden told her. "I'm imperceptible to everyone but you, for some reason. I've been to my house, but my parents, my sister, my grandmother, none of them can see or hear me. I came to look for you after school today. You weren't at cheerleading practice, but I overheard the team and Coach Colletti talking. Did you know they're not going to play in the championship game? Riley doesn't want to quarterback the team, and they're going to take a forfeit."

"I heard the same thing." Alecia felt another twinge of shame, unsure whether or not Braden knew about the conversation she'd had with Riley.

A stray teardrop began to roll down her cheekbone, and Braden reached across the distance between them - which in the mortal world was just a few inches but in the realm that divided them, it was an eternity - and touched the tip of a finger to her face. When he made contact with her skin, an electric arc sparked upward toward the ceiling. The discharge produced a loud sizzling sound followed by a crack of thunder that shook the room. Neither of them moved, their gazes fixed on one another.

"I miss you," Braden whispered. His hazel eyes sparkled emerald green in the hazy, blue glow rippling around him.

"I miss you, too," she told him. She smiled, grateful for being able to share this moment with him.

Braden deliberately withdrew his hand and the sizzling sound gradually diminished. An acrid smell, like charred wood, hung in the air.

"Why did you wait until now to come to me?" Alecia asked.

"It's weird," Braden began. "Time is different for me. It seems like the same day all the time. What feels like just a few minutes can be a week."

"What's it like...you know, being dead?"

"I don't know." He shrugged. "I mean, I can go wherever I want just by kind of thinking about it. That's pretty cool. But other times, I can't seem to control it."

"But I can't touch you," Alecia bemoaned. "It's torture. If we can't be together, what are we supposed to do?"

"I don't know," Braden said. "I'm not sure how much longer I can stay. I don't think I'm supposed to be here. I'm afraid I could turn around and find that years have gone by and you're no longer here."

Alecia's eyes were burning as she struggled to keep them focused on her dead boyfriend.

"One thing you can do is convince Riley to quarterback the team," Braden said. "We can't forfeit the game, Alecia. If they don't play, then my death will be in vain. I think that's why I came back."

"You want *me* to talk Riley into playing?"

"You *have to*, Alecia. You're the only one who can. He'll listen to you."

"What will I tell him?"

"Whatever it takes," he told her. And then he simply disappeared, leaving Alecia to wonder if he had been there at all.

***

Alecia slept well that night, and she woke with a positive, new outlook. She was convinced Braden's visit had been real, and this gave her a perspective and a clarity that made everything easier to deal with. Braden wasn't alive, but he was okay, and that buoyed her spirits enough that she was able to get through all of her classes the next day. No longer depressed or overly self-conscious, she found herself laughing and joking around with her friends. Her jovial mood didn't only come as a surprise to herself. She was aware that some of her classmates were looking at her differently and talking about her. She heard a few snippets of what they said, and she could read body language and facial expressions well enough to discern that some students thought she was callous and insensitive for being happy so soon after Braden's tragic death. Some believed she was an ice queen. Others wondered if she had completely lost her mind, going from one extreme to the other, from catatonia one day to euphoria the next. Some of her "friends" seemed hesitant to talk to her, and those she least expected were the ones to strike up normal conversations with her.

After fourth period, Alecia spotted Beth walking away from her in the corridor. "Beth! Hey, Beth!" she called out over the din of raucous voices and competing conversations, but Beth didn't look up. Bodies moved frenetically in every direction between them. Alecia bodysurfed through the crowd and stepped directly in front of Beth, who fetched up and stared back in silence. Then Alecia noticed Luke Marchand standing beside her. He was a tall kid with light red hair and gorgeous, pale blue eyes. He was looking down at Alecia with the blankest of expressions. If Mount Hope High School had a leading contender for "dumb jock," it would be Luke, the starting center for the basketball team since he was a freshman. He had the body of Adonis and his brains stuffed in his size 14 Adidas sneakers.

"What's going on?" Alecia asked.

Beth shuffled her feet uncomfortably and started twirling the end of her hair. "We'll be cheering for the basketball team now that the football team won't be playing."

"Really?" Alecia said. "I didn't hear that."

"You haven't been to cheerleading practice lately," Beth reminded her. "How would you know?"

"I checked my texts, no messages from you."

"Well, it's not official yet," Beth said. "I don't want to go spreading rumors that aren't true."

The bell sounded, signaling the start of lunch period.

"We'll catch up later." Beth gave Alecia a fake hug, putting both arms around her without making contact. With the pretentious display of affection concluded, Beth and Luke continued down the hallway together. Alecia watched them retreat through eyes narrowed to tiny slits, unsure what to make of what she was seeing.

Beth and Luke?

She felt as if she'd missed something. She'd only been out of school for a week, but it was as though she'd been away much longer, similar to the way Braden described how time passed for him now.

At least the game hadn't been officially forfeited yet. There was still time. She headed for the stairs and went down to the cafeteria to find Riley. Walking into the large hall, she instantly felt the weight of all the eyes on her and heard the whispers of the students seated around dozens of long folding tables. She searched the faces as she passed by them, paying no heed to the unwanted attention. When spotted Riley walking through the crowd with a tray heaped with food, she followed him to a table where he sat down with a group of football players. He looked up at Alecia in surprise when he saw her. "Alecia. Hi."

"Can I talk to you for a minute?" she asked, averting her eyes from the other boys.

"Yeah, sure." Riley stood and followed Alecia, who headed toward the exit doors at the other end of the cafeteria.

"What's up?" Riley asked when Alecia stopped just around the corner.

She waited for two approaching students to pass by before she leaned in close to Riley. "The football game hasn't been forfeited yet, has it?"

His eyes narrowed. "No, but he's probably going to do it today. We're supposed to meet again this afternoon after school to take a final vote."

"Good. Tell them you decided to play."

Riley's forehead creased in confusion. "What?"

"The team has to play the game," she insisted. "You have to be the quarterback."

"Wait a minute, Alecia. I don't understand."

"Braden needs you to do this."

Riley eyes widened. "Braden?"

"I saw him again?" she confessed. "I spoke to him?"

The sound of voices increased as four girls exited the cafeteria and then disappeared down the hall.

"We shouldn't be talking about this here," Alecia said softly. "Let's meet somewhere after your team meeting. Just make sure the game is not cancelled."

Riley sighed. "I don't know."

Alecia glared at him. "You have to play," she said in a sharp tone.

"I just don't know if I can do it. I mean, I know the plays, I know the offense, I just don't know if I'll be able to execute the game plan Braden developed. Centerdale is a really good football team. They're a 5A division one school. They were the district champs last year. One of the best teams in west Texas."

"You can do it, Riley. I know you can. Braden believes in you, too."

"He said that?"

Alecia nodded. More students appeared in the hallway. "Why don't you meet me at the old Granderson barn after you talk to the team," she whispered. "I'll explain everything."

"All right," Riley agreed.

Alecia braced her arms on his broad shoulders and stood on her tiptoes, raising her small frame off the ground just enough to allow her to reach his cheek and kiss him. Riley grinned as her moist lips touched his skin. "I'll see you at the barn later," she said as she pulled away.

He was still smiling when Alecia turned away and sauntered down the corridor. She peeked back at him and waved before she reached the far corner.

***

She made sure no one was watching when she left the school property and headed toward the old Granderson barn. It was a half-mile trek over gently rolling land scattered with dwarf trees and low brush. The entirety of Mount Hope High School was situated on a small, donated portion of a massive tract of prairieland and a mesquite forest owned by a wealthy local family. The barn was in disuse and had been decaying in clear sight for years. Up close, the size of the structure was shocking, with an impressive thirty-foot peak. The prairie barn's long, sweeping gambrel roof came very near to the ground. A machine shed attached to the opposite side was in much worse shape than the barn, with no roof at all and one wall collapsed inward.

Alecia had arrived ahead of Riley, and she ventured inside on her own, slipping through the gap between the double barn doors that were too swollen to close completely. Shafts of afternoon sunlight sliced through the many cracks in the wood-slat walls and overhead rafters, illuminating the dust and cobwebs in an eerie, wondrous glow.

Not long after, the hinges of the barn doors creaked with a high-pitched moan as they were forced open. "Alecia? Are you in here?"

"Yes," he shouted. Dust motes danced in the light at the entrance as Riley emerged, a silhouette cast in complete shadow by the bright sunshine behind him.

"Riley," Alecia called out, hurriedly making her way over to him. "Did you do it?"

"Well, hello to you, too."

"Come on, Riley. Are you playing Friday?"

He was already grinning. "When I told the coach I wanted to quarterback, the rest of the team jumped up and cheered. They all want to win for Braden."

Alecia was beaming. "That's great." She wrapped her arms around him. "Thank you."

Riley hugged her back. "Don't thank me yet. We haven't won anything."

"You will. I know it."

Riley focused his gaze on Alecia. "You said you were going to tell me everything."

For the next few minutes, he listened in silence as Alecia revealed everything Braden said during his last visit, and how he hadn't been able to make contact with anyone else.

When she was done, Riley maintained a puzzled expression. "Was that all he said?"

Alecia thought about it a moment. "Yeah." She noticed that Riley was looking past her with a far off look on his face. "What is it?"

"You know what this place reminds me of?" he asked.

Alecia shook her head.

"Do you remember that amusement park in Galveston, when we got caught in a storm and had to take shelter in an abandoned carnival game booth?"

She was slow to respond. It wasn't an experience she had disregarded, though it was tucked away in a remote part of her memory. It was like suddenly finding something she didn't know was lost. The recollection made her feel good all over. Braden loved roller coasters, and Alecia had traveled with him to amusement parks all around east Texas, often accompanied by their respective best friends, Riley and Beth. Before Alecia had introduced Riley to Beth and the two of them started dating, sometimes it would be just her and the two boys. The Galveston trip last fall was one of those times. That weekend, however, Braden was given an opportunity to visit Texas A&M to talk with the football coach, which he could not pass up. They'd already bought day passes, so Alecia and Riley went without him. They spent the entire day going on all the rides together, from the old wooden coaster to all of the suspended and inverted steel constructions, including Widowmaker, a strata coaster with a precipitous 420 foot vertical drop. By the end of the afternoon, a front moved in quickly and they were caught in a torrential downpour. They got completely soaked before Riley pulled her into old carny game booth. Crumbly cardboard boxes were stacked against one wall. Gray, metallic milk bottles covered in cobwebs had spilled out of some of them. Alecia was shivering uncontrollably and rubbing the goose bumps down on her arms. Riley rummaged around the small shack until he came across an overhead cabinet that had a tarpaulin neatly folded inside. After taking it down and opening it up, he draped it around the both of them to keep warm. They huddled together until the rain subsided. Alecia was amazed how fresh this memory was in her mind. She felt as if they were reliving the moment now.

"You know, Alecia, I really wanted to kiss you that day," Riley said. His face was in partial shadow, but his eyes were fixed on hers.

"I *wanted* you to kiss me," Alecia admitted, and with those two statements all the romantic tension they both had been feeling instantly abated.

"I have another confession to make," he began. "The only reason I dated Beth was so I could be around you more." He shifted forward slightly, his entire face illuminated in a shaft a light. His eyes seemed to be glowing. "I'm in love with you. I always have been."

Alecia almost gasped. It was like being on a roller coaster again; her head was spinning.

Riley pressed his lips against hers. She felt his hot breath in her mouth. When he wrapped his arms around her back and pulled her tight against him, she closed her eyes. In her mind, she and Riley were back inside the small wooden hut in Galveston, wet and cold from the sudden storm. She shuddered, and her skin prickled with a chill as they kissed.

***

The encounter in the barn with Riley left Alecia feeling light-headed the rest of the day. That night, she thought Braden would appear, but he didn't. Part of her was relieved, she didn't know how to explain what happened between her and Riley. It left her conflicted and confused. Over the next couple of days, she hardly talked to Riley at all as he prepared with the team for the big game Friday night. They didn't have a lot of time to get ready, but they practiced hard. Riley was a good quarterback, even though he hadn't taken any snaps all season. He was big and athletic, and he was as much a threat to run the ball as he was to throw it. He may not have been the natural leader Braden was, with the ability to inspire the other players, but he didn't need to be, as they were all highly motivated to win this game for Braden.

On the day of the game, electricity was in the air and there was a growing excitement among the student body of Mount Hope High School. George Donnelly Stadium, on the campus of nearby Cumberland Valley Community College, was the neutral site chosen for the matchup. The weather had been warm and dry all day, but by kickoff it had cooled off considerably. The air had a slight chill, making it a perfect night for football. The stadium lighting was so bright that the field turf seemed to be glowing, with the darkness beyond accentuating the emerald green of the artificial grass and the white harsh marks and numbers of the gridiron.

The Mounties established their ground game early and Riley did a great job leading the offense on several drives. By possessing the ball as long as they did, they limited the opposing team's scoring opportunities. But it was the defense that really stepped up and made their presence felt. They kept the Centerdale offensive attack off balance by taking an aggressive approach, grabbing an interception and forcing two fumbles. Mount Hope ended up winning a close, low-scoring game, upsetting the heavily favored Centerdale Chieftains 12–7. At the end of the game, the players took off their helmets and started chanting Braden's name. A lot of the students, faculty, and parents in the stands joined in as well, and it felt as if Braden was there. He was present in spirit at least, spurring the team on to a thrilling championship victory.

Riley went to find Alecia after the game.

"We did it!" Taking her into his arms, he openly kissed her. "We did it!" he repeated as he lifted her off the ground.

Alecia felt invisible eyes upon her, eyes other than those belonging to her mom, the girls on the cheerleading squad, including Beth, or anyone else who might have been peering at her and Riley from afar. An hour later, the stadium had emptied, only a few people lingering around. Alecia was standing alone near the entrance to the locker room, waiting for Riley to finish showering and changing. The stadium lights were dim, and the field was cloaked in a pall of darkness. The smell of popcorn and overcooked hot dogs that lingered in the air became overpowered by the scent of jasmine and sandalwood. Sensing movement behind her, Alecia spun around and saw Braden standing two feet away displaying a wide, toothy grin. Clearly, he was very happy.

The awkwardness of the moment gave her pause. She didn't know how to react, but Braden wasn't about to leave her on the hook. "I know how you must be feeling," he said.

"Tell me, then, because I sure don't know how to feel."

"Please don't feel bad," he said, his smile not diminishing. "Riley is a great a guy. I want you to be happy."

The sentiment took Alecia by complete surprise. "What?" The word rushed out of her mouth along with all the air in her lungs.

Braden continued to look at her with a winsome smile. "I couldn't leave you without knowing you were okay, and that you were with someone who loves you."

A light went on in Alecia's head. "So, this wasn't about the football game at all?"

"Well, I really wanted us to beat Centerdale, but the game was the only way I could think of to get you two together. I figured it would spark something."

Alecia couldn't believe it. Braden not only knew about them and was okay with it, but he had orchestrated the whole thing. "How could you be sure?" she asked.

Braden titled his head to one side and raised an eyebrow curiously. "I knew he always liked you."

"You did?"

"Of course. He tried to hide it, but it was obvious." Braden gave Alecia his most charming smile. "Easy to understand why, too."

She blushed, which was what she usually did whenever Braden gave her such a compliment.

"You like him, don't you?" Braden teased.

Alecia hesitated, searching for the words.

"It's all right. Really. I don't think you'll find a better guy. I mean, now that I'm gone from your life."

As Alecia gazed at him, tears welled in her eyes. Being able to see him again had played a cruel trick on her mind, and she temporarily forgot he wasn't alive. The same soul-rending heartache she experienced when she first lost him came back, like a wound that had just begun healing suddenly being ripped open again.

"I only want what's best for you," Braden said. "I still love you. I'll always love you."

Tears streamed from her eyes. "I love you." Her lips were trembling. "Will you be able to see you anymore?"

He shook his head slowly. His eyes were laden with sadness, but he maintained a faint smile.

Alecia couldn't help herself and took a step closer to him. A dim pulse of light and energy disturbed the space between them. She raised her left arm slowly, holding her hand palm out in front of her face. As Braden reached for her, there was a burst of dazzling white light. Momentarily blinded, Alecia couldn't see a thing, but when their hands came together, she felt his fingers intertwine with hers. The sensation seemed real enough, and she urgently reached into her jacket pocket with her other hand to pull out her cell phone. She wanted to take a picture. She was afraid she might never see him again, and she wanted something to hold on to, something no one else had. She had to keep her eyes closed to shield them from the blinding light, but she managed to snap several pictures before Braden's fingers slipped from her grasp.

"Alecia?" Riley's voice called out to her.

She continued taking pictures as the brilliance slowly dimmed and then disappeared completely. She opened her eyes. It took a moment to adjust to the relative darkness. Braden was gone and Riley appeared. He took her into his arms and gave her a big hug, which she fully welcomed. Resolved of all remaining guilt, the embrace felt wonderful. She couldn't help imagining one of Braden's hands on her back and another invisible hand on Riley's.

"What were you taking pictures of?" he asked.

"Just some final memories." In that moment, she realized she didn't need a picture. She'd already shared something with Braden that no one else ever would. She didn't tell Riley about seeing Braden that last time or the things they talked about. That conversation wasn't intended for Riley. If it had been, Alecia believed Braden would have appeared to both of them. Maybe someday she would tell Riley everything, including how Braden played matchmaker in fixing them up. For now, though, this was Alecia's secret, something between Braden and her.

She didn't check the pictures on her phone until she got home. It was late. Her heart was pounding in her chest and her breathing was quick and shallow as she scanned the images she had captured. Slowly she began to breathe normally as she scanned through one overexposed photo after another. Only one was somewhat clear. Although it, too, was bright, particularly around the edges, her left hand, with the palm and fingers thrust up, was in sharp focus. A second hand, this one smoky and ethereal, was knotted with hers. The picture had to have been taken at the exact instant when the waning light was dim enough not to have completely whitewashed everything else out, like in all the other photos. The light had winked out of existence right after that picture had been snapped, because the very next one was of the locker room door opening and Riley exiting. Alecia stared at the ghostly hand, and while it didn't appear to be real, that is, not flesh and bone, it looked like Braden's in size and shape. When she noticed the way the tip of the index finger was bent outward at a slight angle, there was no doubt about it. Braden had broken the digit in a game last season. It was on his throwing hand, and he'd refused to come out of the game. He just taped it to his middle finger and continued to play. In fact, it happened in the fourth quarter of a game they were losing at the time, and after the injury, Braden led the offense on a long drive that culminated in a game-winning touchdown.

 Alecia smiled as she stared at the image on her phone and thought about Braden. Just as he had guided the football to so many victories, he had a hand in the direction her life was going. Because of that, she knew he would always be a part of her life. While things hadn't turned out the way she had always imagined they would, she took comfort in knowing that Braden's love for her transcended everything, for there could be no greater example of true love than when someone puts your happiness ahead of their own.

www.ingramcontent.com/pod-product-compliance
Lightning Source LLC
LaVergne TN
LVHW012034060526
838201LV00061B/4594